"You don't belong here."

The stony look in Clint's dark eyes held contempt.

It was a simple statement. One that brought back hurtful memories of all the towns Tess had hoped to call home as a young child, of all the friends she'd hoped to make. She never knew what it meant to stake down roots and build on something.

"And you think you belong here?"

"Hell no. I'm selling the ranch and all the holdings."

Tess tried to ignore the searing shock to her system. Holding her composure, she stared at him. She'd promised his father she'd never sell the ranch. She'd do everything in her power to keep his legacy alive. Not even Clint's intimidating presence would change her mind.

She stared at the man, who had deep-set scorn on his face. "I'm sorry. But that's not possible."

Then Tess lifted her skirts and walked out of the room in a way that would have made Queen Victoria of England proud.

* * *

Taming the Texan
Harlequin® Historical #887—March 2008

TAMING *the* TEXAN

CHARLENE SANDS

HARLEQUIN®

TORONTO • NEW YORK • LONDON
AMSTERDAM • PARIS • SYDNEY • HAMBURG
STOCKHOLM • ATHENS • TOKYO • MILAN • MADRID
PRAGUE • WARSAW • BUDAPEST • AUCKLAND

ISBN-13: 978-0-373-29487-9
ISBN-10:   0-373-29487-5

TAMING THE TEXAN

This edition published by arrangement with Harlequin Books S.A.

® and TM are trademarks of the publisher. Trademarks indicated with ® are registered in the United States Patent and Trademark Office, the Canadian Trade Marks Office and in other countries.

www.eHarlequin.com

Printed in U.S.A.

This book is dedicated to two proud Texans,
my father-in-law Hollis and his wife, Betty.
With love.

Special thanks to my editor, Demetria Lucas,
for her help and support with this book!

Chapter One

Hayworth, Texas
1883

It wasn't that long ago Theresa Metcalf shot her brother dead and put him in the ground so the evil in him wouldn't touch another soul.

She'd loved Rusty as a boy, but her brother had had too much of his father, Frank Metcalf, in him. Rusty had become an outlaw—perhaps one too many beatings could do that to a young child. She'd been more fortunate than the brother who'd become a desperado; her father's wrath hadn't tainted her in quite the same way.

Rusty is dead by your hands, Theresa, she thought solemnly, the memory of that fateful night never far from her mind. But Theresa Metcalf no longer existed, she reminded herself. She'd left Turner Hill in California one month after the shooting and the awful scandal that followed. She'd changed her name and her whole identity, leaving behind her old life as notorious Rusty Metcalf's reclusive sister.

Her dear childhood friend Laura Larson had coaxed her to come to Hayworth, Texas, to replace her position as caregiver to ailing cattle baron Hoyt Hayworth. Laura, her only true friend in the world, was with child and could no longer tend to his needs. Laura had vouched for her with Hoyt Hayworth, gaining her the employment. And she began living a lie—as Tess Morgan, a family friend of Laura's from Oklahoma.

Three months into her care for Hoyt, he'd sent for a preacher to marry them. That was just like Hoyt— pale in color, weak of heart, but his mind as sharp as a bull's horn. He'd given her little choice in the matter, relying on her compassion to grant an ill man's final wish.

She'd buried her husband on their third-month anniversary. Now she faced the enormity of her role here in Hayworth with trepidation at best, becoming known in the town Hoyt had built nearly by his own hands as Tess Morgan Hayworth, owner of the Double H ranch and the wealthiest woman in north Texas.

When someone thumped on the front door like a starving wolf behind a chicken coop, Tess left her bedroom window, where she'd been watching a glorious scarlet sunset melt into the horizon. She picked up her widow-black skirts and sashayed down the stairs. Glancing at the small Swiss clock that sat upon the hall entry—one of the few items she'd taken with her from Turner Hill—she realized the hour and wondered who would be calling this late.

The cook had already cleared away the dinner dishes and was nowhere in sight, and the large, finely furnished ranch house remained eerily quiet. Even when Hoyt had been alive and they'd all crept around for fear of disturbing him, there hadn't been this silence, the deep, down-in-the-pit-of-your-stomach loneliness that surrounded her daily.

She'd been left pretty much on her own since she'd buried her husband. She had no callers. No one came by to offer condolences. No one visited to share a cup of tea and reminisce about the man she'd known for less than a year.

"Greta?" she called out once she reached the foyer, but even the cook that had been with the family since the first log had been split and the first horse had been shod on the property didn't like taking orders from Hoyt Hayworth's new young widow. Though Tess suspected the cook could hear the knocking, she also knew she'd decided to deliberately not answer the door.

The thumping continued, and when Tess reached the door she pulled it open quickly. "Yes?"

She stared into dark, emotionless eyes. The man looked a great deal like Hoyt but for his younger years. Tess drew breath into her lungs in a sharp gasp.

"Mrs. Hayworth?"

"Yes, I'm Tess Hayworth," she said.

He stared at her, his scrutiny revealing an arrogance that Tess had seen before in men she wished she'd never met. His gaze traveled from her eyes to her mouth. He cocked his lips into a smirk before his gaze roamed her throat to her chest.

Tess inhaled. The man arched his brow and continued his lazy assessment. When he looked back up again, his gaze moved to the thick auburn hair she'd knotted up high on her head and then to the few curls that had escaped, falling onto the sides of her cheeks. She waited with patience to hear the introduction from his lips, but instead of announcing his identity, he laughed.

The mocking tone of his laughter cut through her like a sharpened knife. She was reminded of her father and the hardened lines around his mouth, the twist of his features when something displeased him.

"You're Clint," she stated without hesitation. Tess didn't doubt her evaluation for a second. He was the spitting image of a younger, more virile Hoyt Hayworth. Only, unlike her husband, the man at her door had cold, dark eyes and a set scowl on his handsome face. He wore rugged clothes, a tan buckskin shirt that clung close to his upper body and dark trousers that hugged his lower body, leaving no doubt at his power and strength. He didn't bother taking off his black felt hat, making his manners sorely lacking, as well.

"And you'd be my *stepmother*." The mocking was still there, in his voice and in the stance of his body.

"I got to admire you. You managed to nab the old codger before he died. You're a rich woman now, aren't you, Widow Hayworth?"

Clint strode past her and entered the house. After all, it was his house now, too. She'd been told in no uncertain terms by Hoyt's attorney at law, David Heaton, that Tess would share ownership of the Double H ranch with Hoyt's son. Her heart pounded at the notion. She'd known of Clint Hayworth, of course. Hoyt had spoken of him when he'd gotten into sentimental moods. But from what she'd been told, the son hated the father too much to return home while he was still alive.

"You're late, Clint. We had the reading of the will already. I'm sorry you didn't see fit to visit your father before he died."

Clint glanced around the house he hadn't seen for more than ten years as if taking note of things that had changed since he'd lived there. "My father was dead to me years ago. His passing is only a formality."

Tess shut the door and cringed at the harshness of his words. "That's a cruel thing to say."

He snorted and a strangled laugh came through. "Lady, you don't know the meaning of *cruel*."

Tess could certainly argue that point. She hadn't been raised in a big, comfortable ranch house with servants and family who'd loved her. Instead, she'd been a victim of a hurtful man who had taken out his own failures in life on his two young children. Rusty had taken most of the beatings, but Tess had been wounded in body and spirit, as well.

She approached him as he helped himself to a drink from the smooth mahogany sideboard in the parlor. He poured two fingers of whiskey into a crystal tumbler and took a long drink.

"You don't know me."

He glanced at the remaining whiskey in his glass, then up at her with cool eyes. "I know your kind."

Indignant now, Tess moved to the sideboard, her black satin gown rustling in the quiet room as she faced him. "What kind is that?"

"You're a gold-digging whore who married for a bundle and then put your husband in the ground, probably from too many nights in your bed. Hell, I bet you danced on his grave when no one was looking. Can't say as I blame—"

She slapped his face, the sound echoing through the silence.

Without regret for the impulsive move, Tess stepped back. "I know cruel when I hear it," she said, narrowing her eyes, her entire body shaking.

His face flamed with anger for an instant, then he relaxed and put on a smile before finishing his whiskey. Almost as an afterthought, he said, "You've got gumption, lady. I'll say that."

Yes, she had gumption. She'd been on the receiving end of cruelty her entire life. And Hoyt had made her understand that she was strong enough to fight it. Her husband had helped her see that the minute she'd picked up that gun and shot her brother she'd rebelled against the kind of evil that could bring her down. She'd saved two lives that day. With Hoyt's help, she'd begun to forgive herself, and slowly the guilt that had haunted her dreams eased.

Tess vowed to never allow a man to intimidate her again, especially one who made unwarranted accusations. Surely Hoyt deserved better from his son. "You come here and make assumptions about my relationship with your father when you haven't been home in ten years? You don't know anything about him—or me. You may have reasons to hate him, but I know the kind of man he was."

"Yeah," he said, "so do I." He stepped close, and she breathed in the scent of the road on him and the warm night's air.

"My father was a ruthless snake who drove decent people from their homes and livelihoods. He didn't much care who he stepped on to build his wealth. And once he built this town, it wasn't enough. Nothing and no one was ever enough for him."

She shook her head vehemently. "No, that wasn't Hoyt at all," she declared, refusing to believe a bitter son's accounting of his father. Hoyt had been a tough businessman and he'd taught her some of the finer points of running a ranch the size of the Double H, but she'd never believe the harsh image Clint Hayworth portrayed of his father. "He was kind and giving and he cared for—"

"How old are you?" he interrupted. His gaze traveled up and down her body, lingering for a long moment on her breasts. He flicked his eyes up, and she noted a hot gleam of desire he didn't attempt to conceal.

Much to her dismay, that look unnerved her. She blinked. "What difference does it make?"

"Twenty-two? Twenty-three?"

She set her fists on her hips. "I'm twenty-one."

He nodded as if she'd just confirmed the obvious. "My father always had to have the best of everything, the most beautiful, the most *expensive*. And you cost him, didn't you? He paid with his life."

Angry, Tess resented the claim that she might have caused Hoyt's death. Clint had spit out accusations about her that had no basis in fact, but this one was so far from the truth it made her nerves quake. "I tried to *save* his life for months. But where were you? You didn't know he was sick, taking his last breaths. You didn't know your father hoped you'd return home to forgive him for whatever he'd done to you. He wanted to make amends. Now it's too late."

He shrugged. "Doesn't matter."

Tess sighed with resignation. She wasn't up for the argument tonight. She'd gone through the past two months in agony when she'd realized that Hoyt was truly going to die, then dealing with the pain of losing the only man who'd ever been truly good to her. "What do you want?"

The stony look in Clint's dark eyes held contempt. "I want what's legally mine."

"You're entitled to your *half*."

He shook his head. "Not good enough. I want the entire spread."

She bit her lip and drew oxygen deep into her lungs. She'd been told the exact terms of the will and there was no mistake. "Maybe you haven't spoken with Mr. Heaton yet. Half the ranch is mine now. Your father taught me how to—"

"I've spoken to Heaton. I know what's mine. I'll buy you out."

"You want to buy me out?" She hadn't considered Clint even coming home for the reading of the will, much less wanting to buy out her share of the ranch. She'd commissioned the attorney to track Hoyt's son down to inform him about his father's death, but as far as she knew, Mr. Heaton had never gotten a response back. "Why?"

"You don't belong here."

It was a simple statement. One that brought back hurtful memories of all the towns she'd hoped to call home as a young child, of all the friends she'd hoped to make. But Frank Metcalf made enemies of the kindest of people and he'd been driven out of one town after another. She'd never known what it meant to stake roots and build on something. "And you think *you* belong here?"

"Hell, no. I'm selling the ranch and all the holdings."

Tess tried to ignore the searing shock to her system. Holding her composure, she stared at him. She'd promised Hoyt she'd never sell the ranch. She'd do everything in her power to keep his legacy alive. Though she'd come to the Double H as an employee, marrying Hoyt had changed all that. She'd never wanted riches, opulence or the status that went along with it, but she'd always wanted to fit in. Hoyt, though ailing and weak, had made her feel she belonged here. From the moment she walked into his home she'd felt welcomed and trusted. After time, she'd confided in him who she really was, and he hadn't blinked an eye when she'd revealed her sordid past. He'd treated her with compassion and understanding.

She owed Hoyt for that. She'd keep the promise she'd made him. Not even Clint's intimidating presence would change her mind.

She stared at the man with deep-set scorn on his face. "I'm sorry, but that's not possible."

Then she lifted her skirts and walked out of the room in such a way that would make Queen Victoria of England proud.

Clint silently cursed, watching his father's pretty redheaded widow sashay out of the parlor. She'll come around, he thought without doubt. He'd make sure of it. She was holding out for more money. Her kind always did. He had no use for a greedy, heartless woman. She'd just appeared out of nowhere, claiming a friendship with Laura Larson, and had been immediately employed by his father.

Hoyt Hayworth had always appreciated a beautiful woman. Probably hadn't taken her any time at all to coax him into marrying her. Now she was Clint's problem.

Clint poured himself another drink, chasing away shivers of regret. He hadn't wanted to come. He'd wanted nothing to do with his father, his land or his holdings. But Heaton wired him about his father's death and the widow who laid claim to the Double H.

He'd been drawn here by a sense of justice. Hoyt Hayworth had used Clint's mother's money to start up his business ventures, to purchase the land and the cattle. Without her financial backing, Hoyt wouldn't have had the means to build his empire. The cattle baron had used his wife and then, when her health had begun to fail, he'd tossed her away like a rich pile of horse dung.

Melody Hayworth hadn't deserved that treatment. Frail and broken by her disheartening marriage, she'd taken Clint away to live with her brother's family.

Clint lay down on the parlor sofa, finishing off his drink and closing his eyes. He hated this house. He hated everything about the Double H. And he hated his father for ruining his mother's life. And his own.

At one time Clint had been happy here. He'd loved ranching, loved the smell of the earth beneath his boots and the open spaces. He loved growing up with the ranch hands, all the entertaining stories they'd tell. As a boy, the work had been hard, but he'd loved every minute of it.

But one day Clint caught his father in the greatest betrayal of all, and his relationship with him had deteriorated. Clint began to believe every wrenching story about his father's business manipulations and ruthlessness. He'd seen firsthand how his father's faithlessness had torn his mother up.

They'd moved to his uncle's horse ranch outside of Houston, and after some years Clint had become foreman. He built his uncle's ranch into a prosperous enterprise, working with the animals, taming wild horses in his own way. He had a knack for it—and some said it was a gift. When his mother died three years ago, Clint vowed he'd never set eyes on his father again. Though the old man had tried to contact him a few times, Clint had never responded. He couldn't abide a man betraying his trusting wife and child.

Hours later, Clint woke up, disoriented for a moment. It'd been years since he'd dozed in this room. The scents of his youth surrounded him: the musky fibers of sturdy suede, fresh-cut lilies, hyacinth and roses sweetening the air, the hint of smoke from cooled ashes in the fireplace.

Noises coming from the kitchen sparked his curiosity, and he wondered if Greta still worked here. Was she baking her German delicacies before dawn, the way she had when he was a child?

He rose, stretching out his legs. From now on he'd be damn sure to sleep in a bed. He walked quietly into the kitchen, the aroma of rich coffee beckoning. His stomach growled. He hadn't eaten since yesterday afternoon. When he reached the kitchen doorway, he leaned heavily against it and quietly watched the widow Hayworth, silhouetted by golden lamplight.

She stood with her back to him, facing the cook-stove, waiting for the coffee to brew. Her hair, down in long waves, shimmered like sparkling embers of firelight. A flimsy nightdress flowed over her in soft folds, outlining her body. When she turned slightly, her profile reflected delicate features, smooth cheek-bones, a straight, pert nose and plump lips that reminded him of ripe peaches.

Her breasts lifted the nightdress, and in the dim glow he found their shape round and full. His groin twitched at the beautiful sight she made, and he imagined how she'd feel under his palms. Even the reminder that she was his father's widow couldn't bank the urge to take her in his arms.

Wouldn't that be a fine revenge?

Sell the land his father loved.

And claim his widow.

A man has needs, after all.

Clint's boots clattered on the wood floor as he entered the room, and she turned, startled. "Oh!"

Her arms wrapped around her breasts, her attempt to conceal them.

"It's too late for that," he said. "You've got a body any man would want. You can't hide it."

Fury flamed her face, her blue eyes gleaming with anger. "What are you doing here?"

"About to fill my belly," he said, walking to the long kitchen table and unwrapping a loaf of bread.

He broke off a piece and bit into it. "You didn't offer me supper last night. Or a room to bed down in. I slept on the sofa."

She poured a mug of coffee and set it so firmly in front of him liquid swished out. "I didn't think you needed an invitation."

He didn't. He took what he wanted. Dear old Dad had taught him that. He lifted the mug. The coffee flowed hot and smooth down his throat. "Can't sleep?"

She poured herself a cup of coffee, refusing to meet his eyes. "No...I..." she began. "I have some worries."

"You don't want me here," he stated. He knew his appearance on the Double H must have muddied up her plans. She hadn't expected to share the wealth. "Figuring how to get rid of me?"

She scoffed, her full lips pursing together when she shook her head. "You don't worry me," she said quite convincingly. "I'll never sell you my half of the ranch. I owe your father my allegiance. He wanted this ranch to survive him, to thrive and live on. So if you've come all the way from Houston to buy me out, I suggest you go home. I promised your father I'd never sell and I intend to keep that promise. Nothing will change my mind."

Clint stared at her. She was good, he thought. Those earnest summer-sky eyes and her sweet, melodic voice could probably squelch another man's suspicions. But Clint didn't trust lightly. Not any-more. His entire childhood had been a lie. His father hadn't been the man he'd thought he was. Clint had looked up to him, admired him, only to find out he'd been ruthless in his every pursuit, hurting many along the way.

"You'll sell. I can be just as calculating as my father."

Her eyes widened and she appeared flustered, as if something had just dawned on her. "I hope to God you're not the cause of my worries."

With steaming mug in hand, she brushed past him.

He caught her arm, stopping her from leaving the room. He was close, breathing in the scent of lilacs from her hair. Her skin glowed like fine porcelain in the faint light. "What in hell does that mean?"

She balked, fear entering her eyes when he touched her. She appeared like a frightened child, then she took a full breath and her body eased. He witnessed a transformation of sorts, her face taking on a steely resolve. "Don't ever touch me like that again, Clint."

She pulled her arm free.

He blinked, noting the relief on her face. "Who's hurt you, Tess? Was it Hoyt?"

She shook her head. "No one's hurt me."

It was a bold-faced lie. But she masked her expression well, angering him with her puzzles.

He glanced at the alluring nightdress that hugged her curves, then looked into her eyes. "From now on wear a robe. I'm moving in."

Chapter Two

By sunrise, Clint had moved himself back into his childhood room. Amazing how nothing had changed. Just about everything he recalled looked identical to when he'd left. The same blue curtains covered windows that looked out to the barns, stables, equipment sheds and, beyond that, a pasture dotted with wild bluebonnets. His mother never wanted those bluebonnets trampled on, so Hoyt had had them fenced in, protecting them from the livestock.

"He's a good man," his mother would say, looking out at the field of flowers. But Melody had thought the best in everyone and she hadn't seen life clear enough when it came to her husband.

Clint snorted at the memory. Fencing in a parcel of pasture had kept his mother happy so that Hoyt could go about his business without any opposition. He'd give in to her small requests and she'd hold him in high esteem, but Hoyt never truly had made his mother happy when it really mattered.

Clint scoured the room, glancing at the desk where he'd do his figuring in the evening and the bed with the blue patchwork quilt his mother had designed for him. The dressing table and mirror, the pitcher and bowl—everything brought back memories of his childhood, but none more than that last year when he'd lived here and wished he didn't.

Clint plopped his hat on his head and took the stairs briskly, striding out into the burgeoning sunshine. He spotted Sonny Blackstone by the bunkhouse, in his morning meeting, speaking with the twenty-four-man crew. Sonny, the Double H foreman, lived in a house on the ranch, a small place about half a mile from here, and he'd been as solid as the Hayworths' massive brick fireplace he'd helped build years earlier.

Clint waited until the men dispersed, then he approached. "Mornin', Sonny."

Sonny stared into his eyes a moment. "Well, I'll be," he said, his thin lips cracking into a sliver of a smile. Sonny wasn't much on emotion. "Clint." He shook his head. "I'm not used to looking up at you, boy."

"It's been a while."

"Too long," Sonny said, his brown eyes narrowing. Sonny was fifty-five if he was a day and he wore his years of hard work on his face and body, yet he appeared as healthy as they come. "Your pa would've liked seeing you grown up."

Clint glanced out at the acres of Hayworth land,

avoiding Sonny's scrutiny. "You know why I left, why my mother saw fit to take us both away from here."

"Yeah." Sonny stared down at his boots. "Melody was a fine lady, Clint."

"She didn't deserve the way Hoyt treated her."

"Well, I don't claim to know what went on between the two, but you're back now. The ranch needs running, and you're the man to do it."

Clint shook his head, holding his anger in check. "I'm not planning on running the ranch, Sonny. I want no part of this place. I plan to sell it off in small parcels—soon as I get Hoyt's widow to sell me her share."

"Well, that's a tall order, boy." Sonny's disposition changed quickly, his voice stern, fatherly. Hell, at times, Sonny Blackstone had been more of a father to him than Hoyt ever had. "And I doubt Mrs. Hayworth will sell. She's at home here."

"She's got no right here, and as soon as I make her see that, she'll be gone."

Sonny's gaze bore down on him. "You doing this out of spite? I never thought you'd turn out so bitter."

Bitter? Hell, Sonny didn't know the half of it. But Clint didn't put names to his feelings. Most times they just burned inside him like a raging fire. "Don't worry, Sonny. You'll be well compensated for your loyalty. I won't shove you out in the cold the way my father did me and my ma. I'm not as ruthless as Hoyt Hayworth."

Sonny grimaced, put his hat on his thinning gray

hair and sighed heavily. "You sure about that, boy? Because, from the looks of things, I'd say you haven't got half the heart your father had."

Clint watched Sonny mount his mare and ride off, wondering what in hell Hoyt Hayworth had done around here to inspire such high and mighty allegiance in the people surrounding him.

Tess wasn't one for eating her meals in the formal dining room. When she'd first come to the Double H, it was as an employee, and she'd preferred taking her meals in the kitchen alone. Then, once married, she'd spent most of her time eating upstairs with Hoyt, keeping him company and making him as comfortable as possible.

Today she sat at the kitchen table with a full cup of steaming coffee in front of her and one of Greta's delicious fruit-filled Berliners. Usually she refrained from eating the small, sweet doughnuts that Hoyt had loved so much, but today boiled eggs and oatmeal didn't sound appealing.

She sipped coffee as the splintering sound of rapid boots grazing across the floor broke the morning's silence.

Clint.

She looked up to find him in the kitchen, his brisk entry commanding attention. He said nothing to her as he picked up a plate, filled it with Berliners and Brötchen rolls and sat facing her, slamming down a mug of Greta's thick coffee on the table.

He lathered the bread rolls with honey and dug into a Berliner.

"Damn, they taste better than I remember." Clint closed his eyes. His whisper of satisfaction hadn't been meant for her ears, she was certain, but she couldn't help smiling at the comment. She'd reacted the same way the first time she'd tasted Greta's German delicacy.

Clint opened his eyes. "My mother tried making these a few times. She never came close, but I ate them anyway and told her they were better than Greta's."

The sentiment tugged at something deep inside her, thinking of Clint's mother trying to make up to her son for pulling him away from all the things that he loved.

"It's a wonder I don't look like a fat milk cow from eating Greta's food," she said.

Clint noted her soft expression, then scoured over her body with that same arrogance she'd met with last night. "You've got a long way to go before looking like a fat milk cow, Mrs. Hayworth. But you already know that."

And the unguarded moment was gone. Just like that, Clint's remark had told her exactly what he thought of her. "If you're staying here, I'd hoped we could get along."

"I'm staying." He sipped his coffee and stared into her eyes. "But unless you're planning on selling out to me, we won't be getting along much."

"If that's how it has to be. I already told you I don't plan on selling." Tess scraped her chair back and stood, anger rising in her chest. She'd hoped to have a bit of help with the ranch. Figuring costs, writing out the payroll, making important decisions about Hoyt's other holdings in town all added to her worries.

Lately there'd been some disruptions on the ranch. Nothing overwhelming yet, just some things that had started happening since Hoyt's death that worried her. She'd hoped to speak with Clint about them, but now she realized he wasn't going to be much help to her at all.

She brought her plate to the counter and set it down slowly, breathing in the fresh morning air from the open window. The sunshine and vast horizon always helped calm her. She really loved living here on the ranch. Sonny had finally come around to accept her. She felt a friendship with him and she'd hoped that Greta would come around soon, too.

Clint walked to the counter, bringing his plate. She didn't dare look at him—he was just a breath away, and his tall frame and hale body unnerved her. When he set his plate down, their fingers brushed. She snatched her hand away, the accidental contact creating a rush of heat. She rebelled from the sensation, remembering the callous man who was, in fact, her stepson by law.

"We won't be talking about any pleasantries," he explained. "But I plan to do my share around here until I convince you to sell," he said. He leaned near her ear, his lips only inches away, and spoke quietly. "And I expect your full cooperation."

She gazed up into his eyes then, seeing a captivating gleam. He reached out slowly, his fingers gently touching the crest of her cheek and caressing along the slope of her jaw. She stood frozen, allowing his tender touch. There were so few times in her life that she'd been touched with anything other than harshness that she craved a soft touch, even from an angry, bitter man.

"The same kind of *cooperation* you showed my father."

Tess blinked. Instantly she knew she'd made a mistake letting him touch her. She pulled away sharply and banked the trembling of her traitorous body. "You get half the ranch, Clint. And *nothing* else from me. That will never change."

He leaned against the counter, a crooked smile curling his mouth. "If you're issuing a challenge, I accept."

Tess had enough experience with cold, unyielding men to know how to react. She'd been fooled once by Clint's tenderhearted behavior. She'd never be fooled again. And she wouldn't allow him to disrupt her life. She put her hands on her hips and lifted her chin. "It's not a challenge. It's plain fact. Now, if you'll excuse me, I have work to do. I've been running this ranch since before you got here and I darn well plan on running it after you've gone."

Tess strolled out of the room at a lazy pace, while her insides quaked uncontrollably. She wouldn't allow Clint to see her cower ever again. He had to know she wasn't the kind of female that could be bullied into his way of thinking.

Hoyt had taught her that much. And what he hadn't taught her, she'd managed to learn from hard knocks and years of experience.

"It's good to see you, Laura." Tess hugged her best friend as she stepped down from the two-seater buggy. "I'm sure glad you made it out to the ranch today."

Laura's bright smile always managed to cheer her. Tess often wondered how one such person could contain two lifetimes' worth of joy in her heart. Laura bubbled over with happiness all the time and never had a bad thing to say about anyone. Thank goodness for that, because Frank Metcalf wasn't a kind soul and caused a ruckus wherever he went. Yet Laura had remained friends with Tess for the five years that they'd been homestead neighbors while living in Oklahoma. Laura's friendship had gotten her through some rough spots in her young life.

"I wouldn't miss afternoon tea with my dearest friend." Laura's sweet voice and friendly face made Tess forget all her problems. Too bad she couldn't get a daily dose of her. They managed to see each other a few times a month at best.

Tess took her hand and they climbed the stairs that led into the house. "I think Greta's made plum tarts for us today."

"Greta has my undying love. When I worked on

the Double H, she'd make them for me every Friday. And give me a batch to take home to Tom."

"She likes you," Tess said, keeping the envy out of her voice. Everyone liked Laura Larson. Laura fit in. She was a member in good standing in the community. She was married to the editor in chief of the *Hayworth Herald* newspaper, and folks thought Tom a fair-minded man.

Though Greta had been civil to Tess in the beginning, once she married Hoyt, the cook had looked upon her as a freeloader who didn't belong. She made no bones that Melody Hayworth had been the one and only true woman of the Double H ranch.

Tess sat on the brushed-velvet sofa and Laura took the floral wing chair. Greta brought a tray of tea and tarts out from the kitchen. Her ruddy, pinched face relaxed by delight. "Miss Laura, it's *goodt* you are here. I made plum tarts—your favorite."

"Hello, Greta." Laura rose to hug the cook. "Thank you. No one makes a crust as light as you. And is that your special cream?"

"Yes, yes. Vanilla cream." Greta beamed at the compliment, and when Laura sat again, she poured the tea.

"Thanks, Greta. They look wonderful," Tess said, and the cook only nodded before walking out.

Tess sighed. "She's still unsure of me."

"Give her time, my friend. She's worked here for more than twenty-five years. She was especially fond of Melody, and when Clint was born, she coddled him like her own babe."

"She should be in her glory, then. Clint showed up yesterday. He's moved in. Now Greta has an accomplice in making me feel like an outsider."

Laura reached over to squeeze her hand gently. "You're no outsider. You've kept this ranch running and tended to Hoyt all at the same time." Laura leaned back and took a sip of her tea. "So Clint is back? How is he?"

"Rude. Uncaring. He hates his father, even in the grave. Isn't that horrible?"

Laura shrugged. "Clint always had a mind of his own. But when I knew him, he was kind and friendly. And oh-so handsome. I had a terrible fascination with him when I was twelve."

"You did? I didn't know that."

"Tom wouldn't care to hear me talking about it. I liked Clint for two full years. Then I met Tom." Laura's smile curved as wide as a watermelon slice. "It's been Tom ever since." She patted her stomach. "And now we'll be having a little one."

Tess peered at Laura's rounded belly and set her cup down.

Laura giggled and nodded. "It's getting close now, Tess. I can hardly wait to see my baby. I think Tom's just as excited. I'm sure when the time comes he'll write an editorial in the *Herald* for all the town to read."

"Tom's a good man. And you'll make a wonderful mother, Laura."

"Do you really think so?"

"I do. Remember when we were younger and

we'd pretend we were all grown up, married with a baby. You were always so gentle and caring with your baby doll, like she was real."

"The real thing is much scarier, I must admit. And my mama isn't here to help me."

Tess took a seat next to Laura, wrapping her arms around her in a loving embrace. "No, but you have me. I'm not a mother, but I think between the two of us we'll figure it out."

Laura smiled, reassured. "I'm so glad you came to Hayworth and we've remained good friends."

Tess felt the same way. She'd never had a sister, but she was as close to Laura as one sister to another. "So am I. Even though I have to deal with Clint now. He's bent on causing trouble."

Laura's smile remained, but she spoke with quiet regard. "How could he possibly cause you any trouble?"

Tess twisted her lips into a frown. "I think Clint's middle name is Trouble. He's sure good at causing commotion."

When Laura appeared confused, Tess waved off the notion. She had suspicions, but they were, as yet, unfounded. "Never mind. He stampeded his way into the house yesterday, making accusations and demands."

"Hmm, doesn't sound like the young boy I once knew."

"Hoyt would take on a sorrowful look when he spoke of Clint. He was proud of him and regretted what happened between them. If Clint earned Hoyt's love and respect, then I'd say he must have changed quite a bit since then. He's been…difficult."

Laura spoke with warm reassurance. "He'll come around, Tess. He needs to adjust to being back on the ranch. At one time he loved this home."

"That's just it—the ranch represents all the things he hates now, all the things he blamed his father for. There doesn't seem to be anything here he wants, except to destroy Hoyt's legacy." Tess took a minute to explain Clint's intentions to Laura, then added, "I won't allow him to do that. He can stampede around here all he wants, but he won't—"

"Stampede?" Clint's rich voice broke up their conversation.

Tess tensed when she spotted him leaning up against the parlor doorway, listening in. But Clint's harsh tone was gone, replaced by a smooth lilt. The sharp angles of his jaw softened with a rare smile as he entered the room. "Did I miss something? Sonny didn't speak of a stampede."

"Uh, no. There hasn't been a stampede." Unsettled, Tess feigned a relaxed pose and sipped her tea. Without the unbecoming scowl he usually wore, Clint appeared friendly and open, showing his best features, making him even more deadly handsome than before.

But Clint fully ignored her, keeping his eyes trained on Laura. He removed his wide-brimmed hat. "Tarnation, Laura. Is that really you?"

Laura rose and met Clint eye to eye. "It's me, Clint. A little bigger than you remember me."

"Ten years has only made you prettier. I heard you married." He glanced down at her belly. "Tom Larson is a lucky man." He opened his arms, and Laura, right as rain, walked straight into them.

They embraced for only a second, but the sting pinched Tess like a bumblebee and once again she felt like an outsider. She'd never known that true sense of belonging. Now, she was here and the Double H was her home. Nothing would change that. Theresa Metcalf was through running.

"You look well, Clint," Laura said.

"I am well."

"I'm sorry about Hoyt."

Clint shrugged and changed the subject. "I hear your husband runs the *Herald* now."

"He does. He was a born writer. But soon he'll have another role." Laura beamed with joy.

"Well, congratulations."

"We're both thrilled. I've longed for a family for quite a while." Laura took her seat again. "Won't you sit down? I'd love to hear about your life, Clint." Laura glanced Tess's way. "I'm sure Tess wouldn't mind if you joined us for a while."

Clint scratched the stubble on his jaw and looked at Tess. "I'm not so sure about that." He fixed his hat onto his head. "I'd best be getting to work. There's a mare that needs attention, ready to foal. Another time, Laura." He tipped his hat to her. "I'll be around." He strode out of the room after Laura said goodbye.

"Oh, my," Laura said a little breathless. "Tess, he's—"

"Inconsiderate? Rude? Heartless?"

Laura's expression radiated warmth. "He's downright…delicious. Like one of Greta's tarts. You know it's a sinful indulgence, but you just can't help yourself."

Tess snorted, the sound completely unladylike, filled with disgust and annoyance at Clint's ability to charm her best friend.

Laura's bright laughter filled the room. "You have to admit he's appealing."

"Like a cooked goose I'm ready to slice into?"

Laura sank her teeth into the plum tart and closed her eyes to the decadent pleasure. "Ooh. These are good. And you know darn well Clint's no cooked goose. What he plans on doing isn't right or fair, but he must have good reason to believe so. If you two can manage to get along for more than a minute at a time, maybe you'll begin to see eye to eye on things. I never knew a woman who couldn't persuade a man when she really wanted to."

Tess nearly choked on the plum filling she had in her mouth. "Are you forgetting that he's my stepson?"

Laura waved that notion into thin air. "You know darn well that's only a formality. He's older than you. And I *can't* believe you look at him with any sort of motherly concern."

"Heavens, no." The thought was absurd. She'd never once thought of Clint Hayworth in any other way but a man who made her nerves tingle and her heart race. But he made her angry and frustrated with his demands. He wasn't kind or caring, and she'd already vowed not to let any man into her life who treated her with careless disregard. So, no, she'd never entertain thoughts of charming Clint into her way of thinking. "But I do know he'll never be my friend."

Laura took another bite of the tart and her expression was one of sheer joy. After she finished the dessert, she appeared deep in thought. "No, I doubt he'd want your friendship."

"You see! That's what I mean. He's too stubborn—"

"What I meant," she interrupted, picking up a second tart, "is that he's a virile man and you're both living under the same roof. Don't tell me you haven't had some thoughts about—"

"No, absolutely not."

"Tess?"

"Okay, so maybe he's not a stuffed goose. I'll admit that he surprised me when I first met him. He's a younger version of Hoyt."

"And you loved Hoyt."

"Yes, I did."

"I think Clint is more like his father than he'd want anyone to believe."

Tess could only shake her head in denial, but Laura had planted a seed. And if that seed was nourished, it might blossom into something Tess wouldn't know how to deal with.

She'd never been any good in the garden.

Chapter Three

"Sonny, hand me a cloth. This mare's having a tough time."

Clint bent in the stable stall and, taking the cloth handed him, he dipped it into the bucket of water and wrung it out. "Okay, now, girl," he whispered to the frightened mare struggling to foal. "Take it easy."

Clint smoothed the moistened cloth over the horse's eyes, then up around her ears. "Calm down, girl. You're about to be a mother."

Clint looked into the horse's eyes. He spoke with quiet calm, the voice he knew instilled trust in the animals he worked with. He touched her forehead now with his bare hands and whispered softly. His calm, his presence, set the mare at ease. He saw it in the way her shoulders slipped down from their clenched position, the way she laid her head down onto the straw bed, surrendering her struggle to Clint. "That's it, girl. Relax."

Clint scooted down along the horse's flank, skimming his hand down along her side to reassure her. He took a look, putting his gloves on. "She's straining hard. The foal's hooves are pointing up. See the frogs and soles?"

Sonny stood at the horse's rear, nodding his head. "Yep, that foal's coming out backward."

Clint reached in gently and helped guide the foal out, all the while speaking to the mare. "Easy, girl. I've got you now. Stay with me." Then he felt a release, but not the one he wanted. "Damn, the cord broke! Sonny, go keep her calm. I've got to pull this foal out before she suffocates."

Sonny held the mare down, talking to her, while Clint worked with the breech animal, gently pulling to get her out quickly. "Here she comes," he said as he worked with the mare to guide the foal.

Once the foal dropped and was completely free of her mother, Clint waited for a few seconds. "Damn, she's not breathing." She didn't move at all. He smacked her chest once with the flat of his hand.

Then he squatted and lifted her up and over his shoulder, keeping her head down. "Sonny, wipe out her mouth and nose. We've got to let her clear her lungs."

"Here we go," Sonny said, taking up the cloth. He wiped while Clint held the foal steady. "I hope this works."

The filly started kicking her legs, struggling to get down. "We've got her," he said, letting her down before she kicked him upside the head.

The filly wobbled on unsure legs. Clint breathed a sigh of relief.

Sonny slapped him on the back. "Good job, Clint. I don't know if she'd have survived if you hadn't been here." Sonny wiped his hands on his pants. "Ah, I'm getting too old for this."

Clint doubted that. Sonny was as tough as they come, a born rancher. And a damn fine foreman. "I learned a whole lot from you, Sonny."

"Nah, I've never been good with the animals. Not like you. I heard you've made quite a name for yourself back in Houston area. You tamed some of the meanest and wildest stallions, then sold them for a high price."

"Can't deny that." Clint bent over the mare. "What's her name?" he asked, stroking the new mother's mane.

"That'd be Sunshine. I think you've earned the right to name her filly."

Clint looked up at Sonny. "The filly? Can't be anything but…Lucky Girl."

Sonny laughed. "A right good name."

Clint made sure the mare and filly were doing fine before he headed for the house. He strode into the kitchen.

"Something smells awful good," he said, sniffing the air.

Greta turned from the stove. "Clint, what do you do?" she asked, her voice laced with a heavy German accent. She'd been the one person to greet him with genuine affection when he'd returned home. Now she looked at his dirty clothes and sweat-stained face and scoffed, pointing her finger. "And you do not smell so *goodt!*"

Clint laughed. "That's why I'm here. I need a bath. Gotta heat some water."

Greta shooed him out of the kitchen. "I heat the water. You get out of the kitchen. Go! I bring it to you."

Clint headed to the bathing room, removing his belt and unfastening the buttons on his shirt. He yanked himself out of the shirt, tossing it onto a hallway settee, then unbuttoned his trousers.

When Tess exited the office, she turned with a ledger in her hand and faced him in the hallway. "Oh!"

Clint stood, watching her. There were times when he couldn't believe this young blue-eyed, copper-haired woman had been his father's wife. His initial reaction to her always annoyed him. But, damn, she was a beauty. "Afternoon, Mrs. Hayworth."

She glanced at his bare chest, then her gaze shifted to below the waistband of his pants that hung loosely on his hips. Her face colored quickly. The blush on her pale porcelain skin intrigued him.

"What are you doing walking around like that?"

Clint feigned innocence. "I'm about to take a bath. What'd you think?"

"A bath? Then undress in the bathing room." She hugged the ledger against her chest. "You can't…you can't walk around half-dressed like that." She swallowed and glanced away.

"Why in hell not?"

She returned her gaze to his face and spoke with forced patience. "No decent man would do such a thing when there's a woman present. I don't appreciate—"

"Last I checked, it's half my house, half my ranch, and if I want to walk around *half*-dressed, you have no say so. I won't be complaining if I catch you half-naked, Tess. Just return the courtesy."

Her eyes flashed shock. She glimpsed his chest once more. Just having those pretty eyes on him caused a ruckus below his waist. He opened the door and entered before his father's dear young widow saw how much the thought of catching her naked inspired him.

The next morning Tess dressed in her riding clothes—a flowing cream blouse and a buttery suede split skirt—fully determined to clear her head this morning with a brisk ride on her sorrel, Maple. She headed out the back door and walked to the stable.

After her encounter with Clint yesterday by the bathing room, she'd had a fitful night. She'd taken her dinner in her room, refusing to share a meal with a man who enjoyed mocking her far too much.

After his dreadful behavior, she'd come to a startling realization: Clint would do everything in his power to make her uncomfortable. The more she allowed him to bother her, the better he liked it. He had one goal in mind, and that was to buy out her share of the ranch so he could godlessly destroy what his father had worked so hard to build. He would try to wear her down. But Tess wouldn't change her mind—no matter how many times she caught him half-naked in the hallway.

Lordy. That had been a surprise. Tess bit her lip remembering Clint's body, so strong and solid, with muscles that looked like cords of oak and shoulders that spread wide enough to haul those cords anywhere he pleased. She blinked away the sight of his torso and those fine hairs leading a path past his unbuttoned trousers.

She'd spent half the night cursing him silently and the other half recalling the image he'd made, standing there with that insolent look on his face, as if daring her to look her fill and admire him.

She had admired him. His body but not what lay underneath.

Waving at a few of the ranch hands as she passed them in the yard, she halted when movement in one of the far corrals caught her eye—a new filly.

She grinned, happy to see new life on the ranch. She walked toward the corral but stopped up just short of the new mama and her baby, keeping her distance when she spotted Clint approaching the horses.

She watched and waited patiently just behind a shade tree. With his back to her, Clint entered the corral, and immediately the mare strode toward him. He put out his hand, and the mare accepted the carrot he offered. He spoke to her, and she nuzzled up against him. Clint chuckled, a low, deep, earthy sound that was clear and honest with no hint of mocking.

Tess reacted by inhaling a sharp breath.

When the filly sidled up against him with thin but steady legs, Tess could barely contain her frustration. Clint seemed to exhibit charm with every female in the county…but her.

"You through hiding back there?" Clint peered over his shoulder at her.

Tess stilled. She came away from the tree, feeling foolish. "I wasn't hiding, for heaven's sake."

"Okay…you weren't hiding."

She could tell by his tone he wasn't mocking her this time, but he didn't quite believe her, either.

"Come see Lucky Girl."

Tess forgot all about being caught by Clint when she gazed into the big, soulful eyes of the day-old filly. Her light brown coat reminded Tess of warmed cider on a winter night.

She entered the corral and walked over, putting out her hand. The filly stood still, wary of Tess's movements. Lucky Girl shied away to stand behind her mama.

"Just stay still there a minute. She'll decide if she likes you or not."

Tess did as she was told. "Wish it were that easy with people. To just stand there and let them see you mean them no harm. Let them look into your eyes and see your true intentions."

"Sometimes animals are smarter than people. Better instincts and better judges of character." He stroked Sunshine's nose.

"I can believe that where you're concerned. You certainly misjudged me."

Clint let go a *humph* deep in his throat before he turned to her. "I didn't misjudge you."

Tess raised her brows and her voice. "You really think I'm—I'm all those things you accused me of when you first arrived?"

"Easy now, Mrs. Hayworth, you don't want to scare off the filly."

"And *stop* calling me Mrs. Hayworth. We both know you're not saying it out of respect but only to mock me."

Clint grinned. "Should I call you Mother?"

Riled now, Tess lifted her chin and spoke quietly to keep the filly from running off. "Why do you enjoy taunting me?"

"You have what I want."

His voice low and seductive, he looked deep into her eyes, then peered lower to regard her mouth. Tingles of awareness shot straight to her toes. "Do I?"

He turned fully toward her, folding his arms across his middle. He stared at her with those dark, piercing eyes for a long time, making her legs as wiggly as strawberry jelly. Tension sizzled between them. Tess didn't imagine it. She could almost feel the heat coming off his body. Then he lifted a corner of his mouth. "The Double H, Tess. I want your half."

She swallowed.

And was brought back to the moment.

Then anger struck her anew. "You'll never get it."

"I always get what I want."

"Not this time," she said with rigid determination. She turned and walked out of the corral, but something compelled her to turn around.

And when she did, her firm resolve crumbled instantly. Lucky Girl walked over to Clint and nestled her head into his chest as he offered quiet and kind words of encouragement. The filly lapped up his undivided attention, giving him her full trust.

Befuddled and truly in need of clearing the dust from her brain, Tess entered the stables.

She really needed a good, long, hard ride.

Tess mounted her mare just outside the stables as Sonny rode up, squinting against the bright sun. He tipped his brown felt hat, then lowered it farther on his head. "Morning, Miss Tess."

"Good morning, Sonny. Looks like a good day for a ride. I'm taking Maple out for a little while. Mr. Stewart is coming to the ranch to give me his monthly report on the expansion of the Hayworth Emporium at noontime."

"I'll keep a lookout for him."

"Thank you. But I'll be back in plenty of time to meet him."

Sonny nodded, then grinned. "You really should wear yourself a bonnet, Miss Tess. It's gonna prove to be a real bright day."

"Oh, I—" she stuttered, glancing at Clint with the new filly and her mama, "I meant to wear one, but I guess I forgot."

"Hold on," he said, climbing down from his mount. "I'll get you one."

And while he made his way into the barn, Tess couldn't keep her gaze from drifting to Clint, working with the mare in the corral, earning the new filly's trust and having himself a grand old time.

"Here you go. Try this one."

Tess reached down and took the offered hat from Sonny. She adjusted it onto her head. It sat lower than the one Hoyt had ordered especially for her, but it would do. "Thank you. This will work fine."

"It's one of Clint's. But he won't miss it." Sonny winked and slapped her mare on her rump.

Maple took her cue and walked forward in an easy gait, passing the corrals and a watchful Clint as they passed him by.

Once past the houses and outer buildings of the ranch, Tess settled back in the saddle and enjoyed the ride, fully in awe of the land before her. Mostly grazing land for Hayworth cattle, the acreage spilled out for miles. She still had trouble believing all this land was hers.

Well, not *all* hers. Half belonged to Hoyt's son, and she wouldn't forget that. She'd never wanted the land, the riches or the notoriety that came with being Mrs. Hoyt Hayworth. All she'd wanted was to live in peace with a man who'd treat her kindly. She'd had that with Hoyt. And she wasn't ashamed that she'd fallen in love with an older man.

"Come on, girl." She clicked the reins gently, spurring Maple into a trot, the fresh air against her face invigorating. Wild grass and flat plains spread out before her, and the sun beat down, causing tendrils of hair to stick to her neck.

She rode for a long while, clearing her head and calming the riot of emotions that were always so close to the surface. She'd been somewhat of a recluse back in Turner Hill, trying to live her life without incident. But the memories of her father's abuse and then her brother's crimes had changed all that.

She'd had to start all over. Working that out in her mind wasn't easy, and sometimes she needed these private moments of solitude to gather her thoughts. She'd put Theresa Metcalf to rest back in Turner Hill. She was Tess Hayworth now, but at times she just plain needed the reminder.

When she spotted a large cropping of lumbering oaks, the shade beckoned, and she rode toward the trees. Maple snorted and sniffed as they approached the cooler area with sunshine playing hide-and-seek between tall branches. "Cooler now, girl," she said, patting her just below her mane as they rode into the haphazard row of trees.

Maple pranced sideways and snorted again, sensing something amiss in the trees. "What's wrong, girl?" Tess couldn't determine the source of the mare's nervous behavior. She glanced through the shadows and directed the horse farther into the shade.

Two gunshots rang out. In close range. Maple spooked and took off running. Alarmed, Tess tried reining her in. "Whoa, Maple. Stop!"

But the mare flew out of the wooded area and cut across the plains so fast that Tess lost her hold on the reins. She tried for all she was worth to hang on, grabbing for the horn of the saddle. Her boots came out of the stirrups, and nothing but sheer will kept her upright.

For about three seconds.

Then she fell, landing hard on unyielding earth.

"She should've been back by now," Clint said to Mr. Stewart, who stood pacing on the front porch. The man had gone into the house already, spoken with Greta, then come out again. Sonny was nowhere to be found, and when Stewart had caught sight of Clint, he'd called him over.

"Ain't like Mrs. Hayworth to be late. She's been prompt and efficient every other time I've come out to visit. Your cook said she went out for a ride and hasn't returned."

"Don't know what to say, Mr. Stewart. She took off this morning on horseback."

The man stood on the porch, dressed in a striped three-piece suit with sweat dripping down from his bowler hat. He glanced at his watch and shook his head. "I hope nothing's happened to her."

Clint wasn't one to worry, but it was strange that she'd been gone so long. "Tell you what—I'll take a ride out and see if I can find her. You go on inside. Give me half an hour and then if—"

Movement off in the distance caught his eye. He squinted and focused on Maple grazing out on the north pasture, an empty saddle on her back. "Damn. That's her horse," he said. "Looks like she might be in trouble."

Mr. Stewart gazed at the mare. "Never a good thing when a horse comes back without his rider."

Clint agreed on that notion and took off in a hurry to saddle up his gelding. Within minutes he was mounted and heading toward the grazing mare. When he noted that Maple's saddle slanted down slightly off the left side, he knew that Tess was in trouble. Most likely she'd taken a fall.

Once he did a quick assessment and was assured the horse hadn't been injured, he put a hand to Maple's rear end and encouraged the mare back to the stables. "You're okay, girl. Go on back home," he said, nodding his head. The horse took off toward the stables, and Clint watched a ranch hand race up to attend to the riderless mare.

Clint traveled at a measured pace, hoping to track the path Maple had taken. Hayworth land was vast, and he could only venture to guess how far and in what direction Tess had gone. He'd give it some time, and if he couldn't find her, he'd double back and get up a search party.

After traveling for half an hour, a cropping of tall oaks came into view off in the distance. He remembered from his boyhood those trees and their forest-like appeal, granting a cool respite of shade from the otherwise sun-soaked flat plains. Most likely she'd headed there for a rest.

"Let's go," he said quietly. His father's gelding, Midnight, the fastest and most agile horse of the remuda, instantly understood. Already Clint had formed a bond with him, the horse aware of Clint's direction simply by the intonation of his voice.

He was halfway to the oaks when Clint spotted something. He lowered his hat brim to cut off the sun's glare and squinted, pulling back the reins and slowing down. A spot of orange-red contrasted with the dry straw-stained plains.

And when he got closer he recognized the shape of a downed body on the ground. Everything blended into the surrounding hues but that one speck of coppery red, and he was certain it was Tess's long hair.

He rode hard and reached her quickly, dismounting and bending over her. She lay still. And quiet. Blood, now dried, lay at the back of her head, mingling into the tresses and matting the hair down.

He scoured her body for other injuries.

"Tess."

She didn't respond.

"Tess," he said, tapping her cheek. "Wake up."

She made a slight move, then scowled with closed eyes, a look of pain crossing her face.

He cupped her head in his hands and called her name again. "Tess. Wake up."

This time her eyes opened, her eyelashes fluttering as she blinked.

"Stay still," he said calmly, reassuring her. "You took a bad fall."

She looked up at him and spoke in a whisper with soft wonder in her voice. "You came for me?"

"I found Maple out in the pasture."

She continued to focus those blue eyes on him. Today they appeared lighter in color, like a fading winter sky. "I almost didn't see you." He took his hands from her face and gazed at her hair. "Good thing your hair is the color of a Texas sunset."

She took a deep breath, then wet her parched lips with her tongue. "Hold on," he said, then whipped his bandanna off his neck and blotted at the dried blood on her head very gently, managing to clean up the last remnants. "I'll get you some water."

He whistled and Midnight stepped up. He took the canteen and went back to Tess. Bending, he dripped water onto her lips. "Easy, now."

No telling how long she'd been there with the sun beating down on her. The soft blouse she wore had ripped at the shoulder, leaving her arm exposed, reddened now from the intense heat. Her cheeks were sunburned and her skin bore a fine sheen of moisture.

She sipped the water, her mouth opening as he offered her liquid in small amounts. "Are you hurt anywhere else?"

"I don't know."

"Lie still and don't move."

Clint roamed his hands over her arms cautiously, feeling for injury. He lifted her blouse and moved over her torso with finite precision. He was a healer of sorts. Of course, his expertise had nothing to do with people, but he could recognize damage when he saw or felt it.

Right now all he felt was soft, exquisite skin under his palms. He inhaled sharply, reminded of who Tess was and all his reasons for hating her. But she was injured and Clint couldn't ignore that.

He scooted over to her side. "Can you wiggle your toes?" If she had feeling in her feet, there'd be no need to remove her boots just yet.

She concentrated for a second, then nodded. "Yes."

"Good." He rode his hands up and down one leg, then the other. She wore a split riding skirt, and he attempted to lift the lower part to see her legs, but the material was twisted under her and he was able to see only to her knees. "Any pain here?"

"No."

She watched him survey her body, those curious, untrusting eyes following his every movement. He couldn't blame her. He didn't trust her, either.

"What about your back? Don't move, but are you in any pain there?"

Again she concentrated. "I don't think so. I'm just stunned."

"You've been unconscious for quite a while," he told her. "It's well after noon and you've been burned by the sun. No doubt you're not going to feel well for a few days, but I can't find any injury other than your head."

She lifted her arm and felt the bump. "Oh! I do feel that."

"You should. You hit it on a rock and bled some, but that's over and done with. Now I need to get you outta this sun."

"No, I want to go back," she protested.

"Not yet," he said before carefully scooping her. She was lighter than a sack of feathers and fit easily in his arms. "Hold tight."

She roped her arms around his neck, and as he strode toward the copse of trees, her eyes closed shut and her head fell loosely against his shoulder. Her position, nestled up against his body, all curves and woman scents, might have sparked his desire had she not been injured. But Clint didn't like seeing injury to animals—and he supposed that held true even for beautiful, deceitful, stubborn widows.

"Tess, you with me?"

She made a small female sound in answer.

He figured being upright didn't sit well with her, so he hastened his steps until they reached the rows of trees. Still holding her, he reached for the woolen blanket rolled up on Midnight's saddle and spread it out enough to lay Tess down.

He lowered her upon the blanket, then took off his shirt and bunched it up until he had a thick pillow to put under her head. "Still dizzy?"

She opened her eyes and looked at him, the impact of her grateful stare striking a chord within him.

"I feel better now, out of the sun." Then she added softly, "Thank you."

Clint nodded and then looked around, puzzled. "What happened to you?"

"Maple got jumpy."

Maple was one of the tamest horses at the Double H. "Maple doesn't have a jumpy bone in her body."

"She does when there's gunshots."

He arched a brow, surprised by the news. "Gunshots?"

She closed her eyes briefly, contemplating, then the words flowed slowly. "I remember hearing two shots. That's when Maple startled."

"She threw you?"

"I managed to hang on for a time," she said in a defensive tone that made him smile.

His smile seemed to annoy her and she turned her head away. Gratitude only lasted for so long.

Gently he pushed away the hair that had fallen into her face. "You've got two ripe apples for cheeks," he said, then poured water over a clean spot on his bandanna and dabbed her face with the cloth. "This will help."

"Why are you being so nice to me?" She searched his face with a perplexed look.

"Would you rather I pull you by the hair and drag you back to the ranch?"

She chuckled at the absurdity of the thought. "No."

He grinned and they shared a genuine moment of amusement. He continued to cool down her cheeks, chin and forehead as she watched him.

He poured water again and this time cooled her neck with gentle dabs. When he dipped farther to where her collar opened, he glimpsed her soft shoulders and began to dab there, as well, watching her face redden brighter than any damage the sun could do.

She reached for the bandanna and their fingers brushed. "Thank you, Clint. I can do the rest."

He released the cloth and nodded. Seeing her lying there, her riotous long waves spread out and her body prone, for a second he knew what his father must have felt for this woman. For a second he felt true temptation, not created by lust and vengeance but by pure male instincts.

"Stay put and rest a while." He rose and peered at her. "I'm going to take a look around."

And he walked off to search for the source of those two gunshots that had spooked Maple and made her throw her rider.

Chapter Four

Clint returned to her with a frown on his face. That was more like the man she'd come to know. Yet slight pangs of awareness had stirred within when he'd tended to her injuries, his eyes concerned and his touch ever so gentle. He'd given her his shirt to use as comfort under her head, and she couldn't help admire him, the broad expanse of his chest, the strength he displayed, the raw masculinity that Tess thought she was immune to, jumbled up in her dizzy brain.

She'd seen him with the ranch animals. They were drawn to him. They trusted him. She'd never seen animals respond to anyone the way they did Clint. Witnessing this compassionate side of him confused her and made her wary.

"It was a wolf."

"Wh-what?"

"There's a downed wolf about fifty yards from here. Shot twice."

"Oh," she said, attempting to sit up. Clint watched her struggle, standing over her, and once she managed it, he nodded in approval.

Then he offered her his hand. His grasp was firm and tight enough to secure her but gentle, as well. She stood to face him, her head spinning for just one moment.

He held her hand, and she didn't dare release him for fear of losing her balance. He waited with patience for her to get her bearings, and finally the world righted itself.

"Who would shoot a wolf and not stay to help me?"

He cocked his head to one side and raised his brows. "Maybe they didn't see you. Or maybe—" Then he shook his head. "Never mind. Let's get you home."

He bent to pick up his shirt. She grazed over his bare muscled chest once more and took a swallow as she watched him work the buttons and put it on. She handed him his bandanna and he placed it into his back pocket.

Midnight strolled over to him, the horse fully in step with him and his needs.

"Ready?"

She took in a sharp breath. "Yes."

He lifted her up with ease and set her onto the saddle, then in one graceful movement he mounted the gelding. She was close to him, her body pressed to his, and then his hands were on her hips, adjusting her better into the saddle.

Once again sensations rippled through her that she had no cause feeling.

He set his hàt onto her head, protecting her from the sunshine. "I lost your hat," she mumbled, remembering the one Sonny had given her earlier.

"You won't get the chance to lose this one."

His arms came around her as he gripped the reins and spoke to Midnight. The horse took off at a slow, even gait. "You need a rest, you let me know."

She nodded, swallowing past a big lump in her throat. Her head pounded now and it was a real chore sitting upright. They rode toward the ranch, and she found herself drifting off, her head falling back onto Clint's shoulder.

She righted herself.

"Don't fight it," he whispered in her ear. "Just relax against me, Tess. Won't be long before you're in your own bed."

Drowsy and tired of the fight, Tess gave in and let her head fall onto his shoulder. He wrapped his arm around her just above the waist, holding her steady, and at times she felt the brush of his arm against her breast. Even in her dazed state, she thrilled at his touch.

When they reached the ranch, Clint set her away from him, carefully. "We're back," he said, his tone rigid now.

Tess sat straighter in the saddle and thanked heaven that the low brim of Clint's hat shadowed her eyes from the ranch hands, who gazed upon both of them with more than curious stares.

Clint helped her down and immediately picked her up into his arms again, carrying her into the house.

"Greta," he called out. "Mrs. Hayworth is hurt. Bring some broth up to her room."

He climbed the stairs effortlessly and kicked open her door. Walking inside, he carried her over to the bed. When he lowered her, she gazed deep into his eyes, her heart pounding, with a thank-you ready on her lips. She cast him a small smile that he didn't return.

"Get some rest. Greta'll be up soon to take care of you."

He turned and walked to the door, then glanced back at her, his lips cocked up partially. "You want some company in that big ole bed, you know where to find me."

Tess closed her eyes. She'd seen his tender side, and that had surprised her, but nothing staggered her more than the instant flash of desire his last words instilled. She could see herself lying with Clint in her bed, being taken into his arms and—oh, Lord—having him claim her.

She stirred with the unexpected notion, wondering if she'd lost her mind completely when she'd fallen.

The old Clint was back, arrogant and brash.

Oddly Tess felt herself softening to him.

Nothing frightened her more.

Her body ached from the fall and she had trouble resting. Even Greta's broth and chamomile tea didn't help much. She couldn't sleep, her head ached, but she lay in bed contemplating about her life and this uncanny turn of events.

Someone had shot a wolf in the same cropping of trees where she'd ridden with Maple. It hardly seemed like a coincidence. But then, strange things, *small* things, had been happening around the ranch lately. Just enough to cause annoyance and some added costs.

But this time Tess was directly involved. She could have been severely injured today if she'd hit her head harder or had landed in a twisted position on the ground. She wondered if someone had deliberately set out to cause her injury. Maybe someone had wanted to frighten her. But then she had to consider that there had been a wolf in the area and maybe, just as Clint claimed, the shooter hadn't seen Tess at all.

It was a mystery she may never understand.

When a knock sounded on her door, she sat upright on the bed. "Who is it?"

"It's Sonny."

"Oh, Sonny, please come in."

Sonny opened the door and sauntered in, hat in hand, a real uncomfortable look on his face. Tess couldn't remember him ever coming up to her room before, and judging by the sheepish expression on his weathered face, she was certain he'd rather be anyplace else. "Ma'am."

"Hello."

"I'm just checking on you. I, uh, I heard what happened out there today."

"I'm fine, Sonny. Just a little sore."

His Adam's apple bobbed up and down. "Sorry to hear that."

"Would you care to sit down?"

"No, thanks, ma'am." He eyed the softly cushioned wingback chair in the corner of the room as if it were a rattlesnake. "I've got to be getting back outside soon."

She accepted that, wanting to ease his obvious discomfort being inside her bedroom. He was tall and thin and lumbered over the bed. "Someone shot a wolf." She cast him half a smile.

"That's what I hear. Clint doubled back and brought it in. I don't recall seeing a dang wolf that size before. Had a big belly to feed. Must have been preying on our young calves."

"Oh, well, then, it's a good thing he was shot."

"Suppose so."

"Do you think a ranch hand might have shot it? I can't imagine it being anyone else."

"I'll question the men tonight and see if I can't find out something. But don't you worry about that. That's what I came up here to say. You need to rest and get better, and I'll see what I can find out."

"Thank you, Sonny. You've been so helpful to me since…well, since Hoyt passed on. I don't think I could've run this ranch without you."

"Appreciate that. I do. But I'm just doing my job, same as always."

Tess respected his humility, but the truth was the truth. "Hoyt could always count on you."

Sonny lifted his eyes toward the ceiling, his gray-ing brows rising some when he nodded. "That's why I'm here, Mrs. Hayworth. I got years invested in the Double H, and Hoyt, well, he always knew it."

Sonny cleared his throat. The sentiment behind this conversation taxing him, Sonny rarely spoke with emotion to her, but she sensed how he felt about the Double H. It was his home, too.

"Well…I just wanted to make sure you weren't injured."

"Just a bump on the head and some aches. I'll be fine."

"That's good."

He stared at her a moment and she sensed he had something more on his mind. "What is it, Sonny?"

He took in a sharp breath, then shook his head. "Nothing, ma'am. I'm just glad to see you're feeling better."

"Thank you. That's very kind."

He swallowed and put his hat back on his head. "I'd best get back out there. *The ranch doesn't run itself,* you know."

Something tightened in her stomach at those words. It had been Hoyt's favorite saying.

Funny thing how Sonny reminded her so much of her late husband.

Clint poured whiskey into a cut-glass tumbler, two inches high, and looked around the quiet, empty house. There was a time in his youth when laughter and boisterous activity filled the rooms, the ranch hands, smaller in number then, ate their meals inside the kitchen with the Hayworths and they all seemed like one big family. Now Clint could hear the whisper of the trees outside and the eerie silence of the night.

He sipped his drink until he emptied the glass, then poured himself another and walked upstairs to his room.

He shed his boots and clothes and lay down on his bed as memories washed over him—memories he couldn't quite get out of his head.

Painful emotions swept through him. He hated what the ranch represented. He knew that for fact. He hated that his father had put all his time and energy into building an empire at the expense of his wife and child.

He thought of the woman only steps away from his room, the young beauty that had managed to worm her way into Hoyt Hayworth's life. He'd have to fight her to get the retribution he wanted.

And he damn well would—for his mother, as well as for himself. Melody Hayworth hadn't deserved that treatment. Frail and broken by her disheartening marriage, she'd taken Clint away from the Double H ten years ago. He'd been sixteen then, but it had been just a year earlier when everything had fallen apart.

Clint closed his eyes and relived the days that had ended one young boy's innocence.

"Mama!" Clint called out. "Mama, wake up!" Clint leaned over his mother's twisted body at the

base of the stairs. She'd stepped halfway down the staircase, walking on weak legs, before she'd tumbled.

At fifteen years old, Clint wanted nothing else for his birthday but the mare he'd seen run with the pack out on the northern tip of their property. The mustang had been his from the moment he'd laid eyes on her. She'd been wild as the wind, and Clint had tamed her. Eager for his ill mother to see him ride, he asked her to come outside. But he regretted that request as his mother lifted her head and smiled her sweet smile.

"I'm fine, Clint."

Clearly she wasn't fine. Tears sprung from his eyes. "I'll go get Dad."

She took hold of his arm. "No, your father's busy. Just help me to my room."

She passed out then and Clint became frantic. Greta appeared, slinging German words in his face. Finally, once the cook calmed, she ran for Sonny, the ranch foreman, and along with another ranch hand they managed to get his mother back to her room while another man raced to town to get Doc Reardon.

Clint overheard bits of the conversation Greta whispered so hotly to the foreman and he gained the information he needed. He rode Blaze hard and fast until he recognized his father's horse. His mother needed her husband. She was so weak and delicate, and Clint feared for her life.

He stormed into the Stratton home, calling for his father. He'd gone to school with the Stratton boys; Brad was two years younger, and Georgie was a year older. But it wasn't Brad or Georgie he found inside the house. As he rushed through their parlor to the kitchen, he stopped, his eyes widening in shock.

He'd caught his father by surprise. "What in hell are you doing here, boy?"

His father's pants were unbuttoned, his shirt gone. And the widow Stratton was doing all she could to put her arms back through the sleeves of her emerald-green gown. Her hair mussed, her eyes dewy, Clint knew he would always remember with distaste the look of lust in her eyes.

"Mama fell," was all he could manage before riding off angry and hurt, with the wind blowing tears off his face.

"What you saw, Clint—it's nothing. You'll understand when you're a grown man," his father defended after the crisis passed with his mother. "Jocelyn is a fine woman, healthy and giving. A man has needs."

Clint had stared at his father, hating him even more then because, aside from all the ranch hands and employees knowing the truth, he'd realized that his mother knew, as well. He'd seen the injured look in her eyes when she glanced at her husband. He'd seen the longing there. And when she'd had enough of her husband, who'd been too wrapped up in his own wants, too selfish to pay her the attention she needed, Melody Hayworth took her son and left.

Clint had been glad to go. His relationship with his father had deteriorated. He began to believe every wrenching story about his father's business manipulations and ruthlessness. He'd seen firsthand how his father's faithlessness had torn his mother up.

He recalled those early days on his uncle's horse ranch outside of Houston. Loneliness had followed him everywhere. He'd missed the Double H and just about everyone on the ranch *but* his father. He'd retreated from those emotions, finding solace working with wild horses, and after some years Clint had became foreman. He had a knack for taming wildness from animals most thought uncontrollable. He'd calm their rebellious spirit and gain their trust. Some said it was a gift, and Clint couldn't disagree. He felt a connection to them, he shared a quiet calm that the animals picked up on. At times he understood them even *more* than he understood himself.

And now he was back here at the Double H and hoping to gain the ultimate revenge on his father—but first he had to convince his beautiful widow to sell him the land.

One way or another, Clint would find a way to free himself of this place and return to his home in Houston, leaving his old, bitter memories behind for good.

In the morning Clint found Greta in the kitchen, making up a breakfast tray. He grabbed a Berliner, took a bite and chewed thoughtfully, the taste reminding him so much of his youth, when Greta would sneak away several pastries just for him. It's a wonder he didn't wind up as round as a potbellied stove.

"Morning, Greta," he said, taking a seat and

watching the cook spreading strawberry preserves on a thin slice of bread.

"*Goodt* morning." She looked up from her task to meet his eyes. "You want breakfast?"

She poured steaming hot tea into a cup and set it on the tray.

He lifted a second Berliner and took a bite. "I *have* breakfast."

Greta smiled, her light brown eyes crinkling at the corners as she waved her hand in the air. "That is not breakfast. A big man *needts* a big meal."

"Later." He glanced at the tray she had made up. "Is that food for Mrs. Hayworth?"

She nodded.

Clint finished off his second pastry and rose. "I'll take it up to her." He reached for the tray.

Greta grabbed his arm and narrowed her eyes. "Don't cause trouble for the missus."

Surprised, Clint looked down at the diminutive woman wearing a stern expression. "You don't make her feel welcome here. So why are you worried if I cause her trouble? I didn't think you cared about her."

Greta's expression changed from stern to thoughtful. She shrugged. "For Hoyt, I do this, but is not *goodt* to let her know that. She is new here…she *needts* to be strong now."

Even in death, his father inspired loyalty. Clint ground his teeth. "I'm making no promises," he said to Greta. When her face registered disappointment, he winked, and she took a relieved breath.

"You are a *good* man, Clint."

"We'll see, Greta."

He took the tray and headed upstairs. When he reached Tess's door, he knocked.

"Who is it?" Her voice was stronger than yesterday.

Clint shouldered the door open and entered her bedroom. He wanted to see for himself how she'd fared last night. He'd found her yesterday out in the field and he'd brought her to safety. The healer in him would do the same for anyone, he told himself. He'd never preyed on an injured adversary; he wanted her strong and on equal terms when he fought her for his birthright.

Tess sat upright on the bed in a light-colored night-gown, her long hair falling in waves onto her shoulders. A quick assessment told him she'd recovered well. She appeared rested. If it wasn't for her reddened face, no one would know she'd been injured yesterday.

"What are you doing here?" She scurried for her robe at the base of her bed the moment she spotted him.

With a quick grin, he set down her tray. "I see you're moving better today."

"I'm not used to men barging into my room." She put her arms through the sleeves of the robe, and he noted her careful movements. She must be aching by now. That toss from Maple would have left bruises and sore muscles.

"Aren't you?"

She took a deep breath, her annoyance evident from the scowl on her face.

"Greta made you tea and toast."

She looked at the tray he'd set on the table beside her bed. "I'd planned on going down for breakfast this morning."

"It's too soon for that. You should stay here this morning. You'll be stiff as a straw broom no matter what you decide, but you need to rest some more."

"I feel—"

"Like you just fell off a horse?"

"I didn't *fall* off."

Clint shrugged and walked over to the window to stare outside to the ranch below. Already the crew was up; the smithy's fires were burning, the ranch hands rising for their morning meal. Everyone worked together to make the Double H a smooth-running operation. The land spread for miles, the herd ten thousand strong. Today they'd be branding some young steers, marking them for identification.

"I rode out there yesterday looking for clues." He turned to find her eyes on him. "Didn't find much of anything."

"I know. Sonny told me. Why are you so interested?"

"I got an investment in the ranch."

"You're planning on destroying it."

He couldn't deny that fact.

"What about all the people working here? Have you given them any mind at all?" Tess asked.

"They'd be well compensated. They're good men. I'll make sure they leave with a full purse and new employment. It's not about money."

She spoke with rising dismay. "You're right. Because as long as I'm alive, you'll never get my half of the ranch. I won't allow you to destroy my home."

"*Your* home?" Clint's jaw tightened.

"The Double H *is* my home. Whether you like it or not."

He glanced at the tea and toast she hadn't touched and remembered Greta's concern. "Drink your tea."

Her face took on tones of crimson that compared to a startling sunset. "I won't have this argument with you again."

"You won't have to as long as you know where I stand. I won't change my mind."

"I won't change my mind, either."

Clint strode to the door, then turned to see her face flaming. Pretty soon she'd be healthy enough for the fight he'd wager. He looked forward to it. "Put some cool water on your face. Your cheeks are burning."

"Get out, Clint."

Clint grinned and strode out the door before she could toss the hot teacup at him.

Chapter Five

Tess hated to admit that Clint was right. After he left her room, she rose to dress and found the task more than daunting. She'd never been a wilting flower, but she was sore in places she'd never have guessed, and her body rebelled at being put through that torture. Her legs screamed when she tried to step into her gown, and after accomplishing that feat, she had one heck of a time lifting her arms into the sleeves, twisting her body so that she could pull the gown up.

"Lord above," Tess said finally, once the gown was on, but for the buttons on the back. She couldn't imagine trying to reach for those and she wasn't in the mood for Greta at the moment, so calling her was out of the question. "I'm just not thinking," she muttered before she let the gown fall to a puddle at her feet.

A blouse and skirt would have been easier to master, but by then most of Tess's energy was sapped and she felt every movement she made twofold.

Instead of retreating back to bed, she slipped her arms carefully into her robe and walked to the window, opening it and breathing in fresh, warm morning air.

From her bedroom she could see most of the ranch below—barns, stables and corrals. The windmill sat at the right of her view, and close by the water tank piped in fresh water to the kitchen and bathing areas. Hoyt had seen that the Double H had every updated convenience one could have this far west.

She'd been content here when Hoyt was alive and now she'd grown to love her home. She took pride in the Double H and looked upon its upkeep with responsibility and an unexpected protectiveness.

She watched the men gather in the branding area as one young heifer after another was marked with the Double H brand. The scent of scorching hide and the squeals of the calves fighting for freedom had always made her cringe. Hoyt had taught her that ranch life wasn't delicate or easy, and Tess eventually had understood the necessities of growing such a powerful empire.

When Clint came into her line of focus, she thought to close the window and turn away but instead was mesmerized by his appearance in the branding arena. He bent by the calves, stroking their heads, appearing to calm them before the hot iron seared their skins.

She couldn't hear Clint's words, but she saw a difference in the young calves as he held them down and she also witnessed the awe of the ranch hands seeing Clint's effect on the animals.

At one point he looked directly to her room, and their eyes met, as if he knew she'd been watching him. Her first instinct was one of retreat, to close the window and turn away. But she'd never cower to him, so she stood at her window in full view to meet a grin that seemed to split his face wide-open.

"Hoyt," she whispered, "you've got one infuriating son."

She turned away and gave up her fight to stay awake. Her bones ached badly and rest was truly what she needed. Lying in that twisted position on the ground yesterday for Lord only knows how long had drained her of energy.

She closed the thick silk-lined curtains and the room darkened instantly. Retreating back to bed, she lay down, shutting off her mind and hoping when she woke she'd feel a little better.

For most of the day she dozed on and off, only rising once to eat the meal that had appeared by her bedside. No doubt Greta had served her supper, but she'd never seen the German woman enter her room.

After eating half the food on her plate, a few slices of beef and vegetables, Tess drifted off again, her mind woozy and her body still in need of rest.

Secretly Theresa let the bounty hunter in through her cabin's bedroom window in Turner Hill. The man named Bodine had come to rescue the young girl he'd been hired to protect, Emma Marie Rourke. The girl had been playing a dangerous game with Theresa's outlaw brother, Rusty, trying to secure her release, and Theresa knew there'd be trouble. Rusty wanted the bounty hunter dead and he'd use an innocent young woman to his gain. He'd tricked Emma Marie into coming here, and Theresa knew the young woman was as good as dead, as well.

Rusty held Emma Marie tight. "I've got a gun pointed at the little lady's head," he said with a mean look in his eyes. "I'll shoot her."

"You won't get the chance," Bodine said. "Your men are in custody. The marshal and his deputies are right outside the door. You hurt one hair on her head, you're a dead man. Now drop the gun and turn around."

Rusty hesitated and Bodine cocked his shotgun. The chilling sound stopped Rusty instantly. He dropped his weapon.

"You gonna shoot me when I turn around?" Her brother's voice sounded faint and weak.

"Maybe," Bodine said between tight lips, his whole body trembling with hatred.

Rusty fell to the floor, great sobs escaping his throat. "Don't kill me," he pleaded, his back still to Bodine. "I'm begging, don't shoot!" Then with one swift, unexpected movement, Rusty grabbed a knife from under the rug and turned quickly, ready to throw the dagger.

Theresa lifted her revolver and squeezed the trigger. She couldn't let him kill again. She couldn't.

Her brother fell forward with the knife still clutched in his hand, a look of shock on his face before he keeled over.

"I'm sorry. I'm sorry," Tess cried, waking up startled, her body shaking. "Couldn't let you kill again," she pleaded in the dark. "I couldn't let you hurt anyone else." She thrashed back and forth, reliving that horrible scene. Disoriented, with those vivid images still playing in her head, slowly Tess regained some composure. She reminded herself that her brother had had no remorse, no humanity in his soul. Her brother had killed and would have killed again if she hadn't stopped him. She had saved two innocent lives that night.

But sometimes she'd think of Rusty in their youth, when their father's ways hadn't yet turned her brother mean and cruel. She'd think of him innocently playing outside, racing off to hide, hoping she wouldn't find and tag him in their silly game.

When she thought of him that way, her heart ached so much it sickened her for the loss of their youth. Those bittersweet memories lingered, and, sadly, Rusty hadn't been that lovable boy for very long.

She'd had nightmares before she'd married Hoyt but not since. Not until tonight. After she'd seen Clint.

She wouldn't credit him with too much. She'd taken a terrible fall yesterday. Maybe the trauma to her head and body had caused these hurtful memories to come back.

Memories she'd never forget.

Tess left her bed and poured rose-scented water onto a cloth. Dabbing her face and neck, she refreshed herself with the cooling water and the floral scents. Still reeling from the nightmare, she paced the floor. Night had descended onto the ranch, and all was quiet but the pounding of her heart.

She found resting today had eased her achy limbs and restored her energy. Wide-awake now, she opened her curtains, and moonlight streamed inside, illuminating the room enough for her to dress into a skirt and blouse easily. Pulling her hair back in a yellow ribbon, grabbing a shawl and tidying herself a bit, she exited the room and strode down the stairs.

Restless now after spending the entire day sleeping on and off, she didn't know what she wanted to do or where she would go. She only knew she needed some fresh air.

Wrapping her shawl around her tightly, she walked out the front door and her attention was immediately drawn to the water tower. She heard strange noises coming from that direction. Tess struggled to determine the cause of those sounds, and when she couldn't rightly figure it out, she grabbed a lantern from the house and headed that way.

She walked past the quiet bunkhouse, past the stables and beyond that, where only the muffled sound of Bucky Shelton's sheepdog's snoring reached her ears.

From behind, a gloved hand covered her mouth. Startled, she stiffened with fear.

"Shhh," the man whispered in her ear, grabbing her around the waist and moving her across the yard, back toward the barn.

Tess kicked him in the shins and he muffled a vile curse. Once he got them both to the side of the barn, Clint pressed up against her back, refusing to let her see him. "Quiet, Tess. It's Clint. Now I'm gonna let go and you can turn around. I need you to listen. Agreed?"

She hesitated, then nodded, her body shaking.

Once he released her slightly, she whirled around, yielding the lantern like a flaming weapon. He caught it before she could knock him upside the head. Grabbing her wrist, he wrestled the lantern free and doused the light rapidly. "Damn it, Tess!" He'd muffled his voice, but couldn't bite back his temper.

"What are—"

He put a finger to her lips. "Shhh!" he whispered. "There's someone out there by the water tower, and I'm damn sure they weren't relieving themselves up against the post. I don't know who or what, but I planned on finding out before you came trotting outta the house, scaring them off. Now are you gonna quiet down?"

Her eyes flashed blue lightning. Then she nodded.

He took his finger away and stared at her. All he could see was the outline of her face and the glow of anger in her eyes. But he could smell the scent of flowers, soft and light, wafting up and chasing away harsh barn odors.

He braced his hands on the wall on either side of her, trapping her there until he was sure they were both safe.

"I heard sounds from the water tower, too," she whispered.

"I saw you heading there. Whoever it was is most likely gone by now."

Her chest moved up and down and she trembled, but Clint only felt the press of her breasts on him. His groin reacted instantly. Tess Morgan Hayworth was a beautiful woman, and even though they were adversaries, he couldn't deny his attraction to her.

He supposed he should back away, but when had he ever intentionally backed away from a pretty woman?

"Scared?" he asked.

"Should I be?" she whispered back.

Clint's brows rose and he smiled. She clearly hadn't gotten his true meaning. He looked at her mouth, set in an alluring pout, and considered his options. He should kiss her into oblivion and be done with it. Ease his powerful curiosity some. "I think so."

"I'm not afraid of anyone…*anymore.*"

He lowered his head, ready to prove her wrong. She *should* fear him. She should be wary of his intentions.

Just as he brought his lips to hers, she shoved at his immovable chest. "No," she said softly, without much resolve.

Clint lifted a hand to her delicate throat, caressing the skin there with a finger and wishing he'd taken off his work gloves. "Are you sure about that, Tess?"

She swallowed, her throat moving up and down, and he caught the hesitation in her eyes. "I'm sure… let me go."

He lifted his hands from her and backed up a step. Though she spoke decidedly about not fearing anyone, Clint didn't believe her. She'd been hurt and she'd been frightened in her life. He admired her struggle for strength, but he hardly believed that she feared no one.

Those scars didn't heal easily or quickly.

Clint knew that for fact. "Go back inside. I'll check out the water tank."

"No," she said, and he heard the stubborn tone in her voice. "I'm going with you. It's my ranch, too, Clint. I need to know what's going on."

He shrugged. "Fine by me." He grabbed the lantern, turned it back on and took her hand, leading her briskly toward the windmill and the tank of water that supplied the house and ranch.

Even before they arrived there, the damage was clearly apparent as they sidestepped watery puddles forming at their feet. Water had seeped out of the tank by three punctures made in the huge metal barrel. It had taken someone a good deal of effort to etch out a depression and poke the large holes.

Clint left Tess standing just a few feet away and made a closer inspection, using the lantern to illuminate the area. "Someone knew what they were doing. They poked enough holes to empty the tank in just a few minutes. These metal tanks aren't easy to repair.

It'd take a few months to get a new one from back east. I'll get the smithy on it first thing in the morning. He'll patch it, but I don't know if it'll hold."

"Who would do this?"

Clint turned to look at her. "My guess is that someone is sabotaging the ranch."

"But why?" Then a light flickered in her eyes. "You were the only one out here. And you came upon me so quietly that I never heard you. For all I know, you were the one poking those holes."

"And why would I do that?" Clint's sharp reply only brought on more suspicion.

She took a step toward him, unmindful of the water spreading out across the yard, muddying the ground and dirtying up her skirt edges and boots. "To wear me down. To make things hard around here. It's no secret you're out to ruin the ranch."

"I plan to sell off the land, not destroy it."

For a second he might have convinced her, but then her blue eyes narrowed on him, and she gave him a shake of her head before she turned and walked away.

"Hell."

With hands on hips, Clint watched her leave. He shouldn't care that someone was sabotaging the ranch, if that were truly the case, but there was something niggling at him. He didn't like being made a fool. He didn't appreciate being tricked and he wasn't entirely sure that lives wouldn't be in danger. Tess's fall yesterday wasn't an accident. He was convinced there was more to that story, but he couldn't figure it out just yet.

At the moment he was half owner of the Double H and he'd be damned if he'd allow anyone to foil his plans for revenge. Let Tess think what she would. It didn't matter whether she believed him or not.

But one thing was for sure: he'd get to the bottom of it.

Clint rose early the next morning and walked over to the smithy's open shed. The constant smell of smoke, fire and ash put the blacksmith's work area far away from the house and outer buildings. Gabriel Whorley worked alone and he was new to Clint, though he'd been with the Double H for six years now. Sonny vouched for him, claiming him an expert craftsman. And a good smithy was valuable and as essential to a ranch the size of the Double H as the longhorns themselves.

"Morning, Gabe," Clint said once he spotted the smithy setting up his tools.

"Oh, morning, Mr. Hayworth." He walked out of the covered area, squinting into the early sun. Then he grabbed his hat and plopped it onto his head.

Clint scanned the shed and the tools the smithy used, noting that Gabe kept things orderly. "We had some trouble last night. Seems someone poked some big holes in the water tank. Flooded the ground and most the water is gone. Gonna take a while to fill it again. That's if you can rig up something to repair it."

Gabe scratched at his dark beard. "I've never repaired a tank before. I'll take a look-see and let you know what I can do. That tank was special-ordered by Mr. Hayworth before I got here. I imagine it's hard to replace."

"It is," Clint agreed.

"Who'd you think would do something like that?"

Clint shook his head. "Don't know exactly. Did you see or hear anything unusual yesterday? See anyone that didn't belong on the ranch?"

Gabe thought on it for a second, then shook his head. "No, sir. No one came around here much yesterday. I spent the day making up shoes for Sonny's horse. He's about the only one I saw yesterday around here."

"Okay," he said, then he walked closer to the smithy's work area. "Anything missing here from your tools?"

"Missing?" Gabe's furry brows rose in surprise. He looked around and made a quick assessment. "No, sir. I don't see anything missing."

Clint nodded. "Just thinking that someone would need some powerful tools to puncture the tank."

"An ax would do it."

Clint shook his head. "No, they weren't ax marks."

Gabe stroked his beard again. "I'd best go see what exactly happened."

Clint walked with him over to the tank, and they marched right through the mud that was slowly beginning to dry up from the sun's heat.

Gabe noted the puncture marks and made an instant assessment. "Seems they used a long metal pole, pointed at the tip, and hammered at it until it went through. A big metal stake would make a hole that size."

"You make any metal stakes that size lately?"

"No, sir. I'd have no cause to make a stake that size. Are you accusing me of something, Mr. Hayworth?"

Clint glanced at the man bearing pride and defiance in his eyes. From what he knew about Gabe Whorley, he was a family man. Had a wife and two boys who lived in a nice little house in town. He'd never gotten himself in any trouble, and Clint had no reason to suspect him. "No, Gabe. Just trying to figure out this mystery."

The man's stance relaxed and he took off his hat to scratch his head. "Don't suppose I can figure it either."

"Do you think there's anything to be done about it?"

Again Gabe peered up at the water tank and thought for a minute. "I got me a few ideas. Something like a barrel hoop might work. 'Course, I've never made a hoop that size before, but I'll get to work on it straightaway."

Clint drew in a breath. "Thanks. Let me know your progress."

"Yes, sir."

Gabe headed toward his shed while Clint walked back toward the house. Sonny rode up then and Clint met him by the stables.

"Mornin', Clint."

"Sonny," he said, watching the older man dismount. He was just shy of his father's age, but

Sonny was the picture of health, weathered a bit by hard work on the ranch but as energetic as a man half his age. "We've got us a problem."

After Clint finished explaining about the water tank and his suspicions about Tess's fall the other day, Sonny took on a serious tone. "Someone's out to hurt this ranch. But they're doing it little by little. Sure don't know what's to come next."

"Right. That's why I think we should post guards around the ranch night and day."

Sonny's face registered shock. "Guards?"

"That's what I said."

Sonny removed his hat and winced at the sunshine beaming down on him. "I don't think that's necessary."

"Why the hell not?"

"Why do you care anyhow? You're fixing to sell off this place if you ever convince Mrs. Hayworth to let you buy her out."

"I *don't* care. But what I do with this ranch is going to be on *my* terms, not whoever's doing this."

"So you haven't changed your mind?"

"No, Sonny. I haven't changed my mind. I'm still planning on breaking up the Hayworth empire, such as it is."

"You hate your father that much?"

Clint stared at Sonny, bitterness seeping in. Yes, dammit, he still hated his father. All he had to do was think of his mother's heartache, the way she died, so sad and lonely, and the feelings stirred in his gut like a witch's unsavory brew. "What do you think about the guards?"

Sonny shook his head. "I think we should wait on that. Armed guards around the ranch will only make the men jumpy. We've always watched out for one another. I'll talk to the men and have them report back if they see anything unusual. But I'm saying no guards on the ranch. Not now."

Clint stewed on that for a minute. He'd always trusted Sonny's opinion. "Okay," he said. "We'll wait. But you make sure the crew knows to keep an eye out for anything suspicious."

Sonny nodded and strode off.

Clint headed toward the house with an odd feeling in his gut. He didn't want any sentimental feelings for the ranch wedging their way inside. The Double H wasn't his home any longer.

He'd be better off gone from here.

But not before he did what he'd set out to do.

He'd been too dang soft on Tess Hayworth. It was time to put pressure on her to sell out. She'd recovered from her injury, and now he'd meet her on equal terms.

Chapter Six

Clint barged into the study unexpectedly and set Tess's nerves on edge with his impatient tone. "What's it gonna take for you to give up the Double H?"

She set her pen down on Hoyt's solid mahogany desk, closed the payroll books she'd been working on and stared at him. Last night he'd nearly kissed her, and she'd been momentarily tempted. He'd been kind and caring when he'd rescued her out on that field, and for one moment last night she'd remembered how that felt. His hands had been tender on her, his voice soothing. She'd felt safe and protected while she was with him that day; his need to see her safely home had touched her deeply.

There was compassion inside him somewhere, and, sadly, he saved it only for the animals he worked with. Last night she'd fought the temptation when his breath had caressed her face, his mouth hovering so close to hers. She couldn't trust him. She knew of his plans so she'd prevented the kiss from happening once common sense had taken hold. And now he stood in the study like a bull ready to charge, nostrils flaring, and expecting her to cow to his will.

"Take?"

"I want outta here—the sooner, the better. But you damn well know I can't leave here until you sell me your half of the ranch."

Tess rose from her seat and faced him, the desk between them. "You can leave here anytime you'd like."

He scoffed and drew a deep breath. "You'd like that, wouldn't you?"

She cast him a polite smile. "You don't know how much."

His brows furrowed together and he took on a look of great annoyance. "You want it all, don't you? But why be saddled with the problems the ranch is having? You're a beautiful woman. You can make a good life for yourself without all these worries. How much is it going to take, Tess? I can offer you—"

"I don't want your offers, Clint. I've already told you that. You're not getting my half of the ranch. This is my home now. I made a pledge to your father and I'll never give in to your demands."

Clint leaned in, bracing both hands on the desk, and met her gaze squarely. "You're a fool, Tess."

"I've been called much worse names. Some of them by you." She arched one brow, daring him to deny it.

He studied her with dark, piercing eyes. "I don't

get it. Is it the power? Do you like being Hoyt Hayworth's widow?"

"No! I wish your father hadn't died. He was a good man."

"Obviously you didn't know him well."

"I knew him *very* well."

Clint straightened, his form rigid, and he surveyed her up and down, his gaze traveling over her body with slow deliberation, a hot, steamy gleam in his eyes. "You knew a sickly old man, Tess. No doubt my father enjoyed you, but it couldn't have been all that thrilling for you, bedding a man with half his body in the grave."

Tess abhorred violence of any kind. She wouldn't slap him again—once had been quite enough and a mistake, though he had no right speaking those cruel, filthy words. She closed her eyes briefly, then with new resolve tidied up the desk before addressing him directly. "I think we're through here. There's nothing more to say. Excuse me, I have a meeting in town this morning."

She strode out the door and decided right then and there she'd not engage in battle with Clint ever again. His accusations and demands would go on deaf ears. It'd do her good to have a day away from the ranch and the insufferable man who managed to insult and irritate her every time they spoke.

When the weather was bad, the meetings were held in a small private room in the *Hayworth Herald* office.

But on days such as today, when only slight breezes blew by and sunshine was in abundance, Tess preferred to have these meetings outside, by the stream half a mile away from the church grounds. Bluebonnets bloomed along the quiet waters and made a comfortable cushion for the blankets Tess laid down. She'd brought a basket of muffins and sweet breads from home and sat down, handing Pearl Cowper a sugary apple muffin. "Please have one, Pearl."

"Oh, no, thanks, ma'am," Pearl said. "I can hardly eat when I come to these meetin's. My stomach's in knots this mornin'."

Tess calmed her with a gentle hand on her arm. "You're brave for coming, Pearl. And you're not doing anything wrong by meeting me here." Then Tess looked at eighteen-year-old Marla McKee. "Both of you ladies are brave and strong."

She offered Marla a muffin, and the girl took one, holding it in the palm of her hand, her eyes downcast. "It's just that I'd be in a pack of trouble if my father knew that I was talking about him in such a way."

Tess looked Marla over carefully. There were no new bruises on her face, but that didn't mean that her father hadn't hit her recently. Sometimes the bruises were hidden, but the emotional scars stayed for years and years.

"Ralph would knock me to hell and back if he knew I was here, Mrs. Hayworth. My husband keeps things to himself, but I feel I got to be here. I can't take much more," Pearl said, and Tess's heart went out to her.

Just some years ago, Tess had been in the same predicament, controlled by a violent, cruel man. Her father hadn't shown much mercy on Rusty. Her brother had been slapped around, beaten many times until his face bore resemblance to a ripe tomato, but her father had been abusive to her, as well. She'd always believed Rusty had taken the brunt of the beatings, leaving her father satisfied to hit her only occasionally. Yet his verbal taunts and his cold, unforgiving nature had left their mark on her in other ways.

"You're nothing but a stupid excuse for a girl. Now get over here and feed me that slop you call supper."

After so many times being called stupid, ignorant and ugly, she'd begun to believe it. She'd believed she wasn't worth the cost of the clothes on her back—another thing Frank Metcalf would snarl at her on a daily basis.

Tess couldn't allow Pearl and Marla to continue to go through that, believing the worst about themselves and living in fear every day. This was their fifth meeting. And when Tess couldn't make it into town, Laura would come, just to listen.

Tess recalled how much she'd wanted to tell someone of her father's wicked ways. But she'd never dared. She'd lived in constant dread of him. Now Tess found a way to help others by listening and offering comfort and hope.

She had a plan to do more. To help other women in the same situation. But she was the first to agree that it was complicated and there wasn't always an easy solution.

"You both know that I'm listening to you because I've had my share of hard times when I was younger. My father was a cruel man. I understand what you're facing now. Back then, I wished I had someone to tell, someone who could just listen to me. The injustice done to you is unforgivable. And my offer still stands, ladies. If you ever want my help in any other way besides to listen, I'm here. You're welcome at the Double H ranch anytime."

"I'm scared, Mrs. Hayworth," Marla said, her body shaking. The young girl lived in dread of her father's wrath. Something Tess could certainly relate to.

"I'm not so scared of Ralph anymore. I figure if he kills me, he'd be puttin' me outta my misery. Ralph don't have a clue about cookin' or house tendin'. He'd be in a bad way and I'd get my revenge from the grave."

Alarmed, Tess shook her head. "No one is going to die, Pearl. But I do understand your desperation."

As bad as her father had been, Tess had never gotten to the point that she'd wished herself dead. Pearl had taken abuse by her husband for too many years. It was time it stopped.

"Seems to me there's nothin' to be done about it."

The dejection and heartache in the woman's voice prompted Tess to say what had been on her mind for weeks now. There was something to be done about it, but it required a good deal of courage on Pearl's part.

"There *is* something we can do. We can have our meetings in public. Start a group for all the women in Hayworth and surrounding towns."

"No!" both women chorused at once, each with a look of distress on her face.

"Now hear me out," Tess soothed, fully aware of their apprehension. "It's something to think about." Tess had never wielded her power as a Hayworth before, but she'd be willing to do so for this cause. "Pearl, your husband works for Hayworth Freight. And, Marla, your pa works at the Emporium."

They eyed her suspiciously before nodding. There were five major Hayworth holdings in town: the freight company, the store, the newspaper, the livery and the hotel. In all, Hayworth employed a good many people in town, and others were beholden to Hoyt Hayworth in some way. "What if I sent out invitations to all the females related to Hayworth employees to come to a women's meeting. Only it wouldn't be a social gathering but more of a discussion group."

"Our men wouldn't let us go, mostly," Pearl said. "I have to lie my way here every week, Mrs. Hayworth."

"You wouldn't be given a choice. My invitation would make it clear that you'd be expected to come. Being Mrs. Hoyt Hayworth has its advantages, ladies."

"Are you saying you'd make threats?" Marla's innocent eyes went wide with a bright gleam.

"Not so much threats, but your pa would insist you come. He wouldn't want you to miss it."

"But how's that gonna help?" Pearl asked. "I won't be speaking of this in front of the town's women, Mrs. Hayworth. If Ralph got wind of it, I'd be asking for an early grave for sure."

"We'll take it one step at a time. There may be more women in the very same situation. I want to find them and listen to them. I do have a plan, ladies. Are you willing to trust me?"

The women looked at each other first, then they both nodded.

"I trust you, Mrs. Hayworth." Marla spoke with conviction. "I know there's at least one more woman who's claiming to fall down a lot. She shows up with bruises at church sometimes. I know her. She's not that clumsy."

Pearl was a little more hesitant. "This ain't gonna cost Ralph his job, is it, Mrs. Hayworth?"

"It's not my intention, Pearl." Yet Tess knew that Pearl couldn't stop the abuse on her own. Her husband needed an incentive. "If you're not willing to do this, then we can continue on with our meetings just as they are."

Pearl cast her a thoughtful look. She sighed and took a breath. "I'm trusting you, Mrs. Hayworth. Ralph ain't changing for me, that's for dang sure. Maybe there's something you can do."

"I'll be honest with you—sometimes the meanness is wedged too deep inside to change a man. That's how it was with my pa. But if there's any good inside, maybe we'll find it."

"Ralph used to be so kind to me, when we was younger. He got mean when we lost one child after another before they was born. I'm sure he blamed me."

Tess took hold of both of Pearl's hands and squeezed gently. "I'm so sorry. Losing an unborn child is hard, but to lose many must have been unbearable. You're strong, Pearl. You've endured a great deal."

Pearl's eyes misted with tears. "I don't feel strong at all anymore."

"You're stronger than you think." She turned to the younger girl and cast her a reassuring smile. "And so are you, Marla. You must believe that. It took me a long time to realize that about myself. Why, it wasn't until my late husband convinced me of it before I believed that about myself. Now I hope to make you both see that you have genuine worth in this world."

"Thank you, Mrs. Hayworth." Pearl squeezed her hand once before standing up. "I'd best get back home now."

"Yes," she said and both she and Marla bounded up, as well. "I think we've accomplished something here today. Go home, ladies. I'll be contacting you again soon."

After the ladies walked off, Tess picked up the blankets and the basket, then gazed out at the quiet stream with a small sense of relief. Today she had achieved something worthwhile and a plan had taken hold.

And if nothing else, she believed she'd given the two women something she'd never had during those bad times in her life.

Hope.

She took her time walking back into town, enjoying the morning and formulating just the right words in her mind for the invitations she'd send out. Once she reached the *Hayworth Herald*, she entered the office and found Tom, with spectacles on, deep in concentration at his desk.

"Am I interrupting?" Tess said, peeking over his shoulder. He hadn't heard her come in.

If anyone was meant to be a newspaperman, it was Tom Larson. His dedication and talent for putting out the *Hayworth Herald* on time every week was unequaled. It was something Hoyt had insisted upon. He'd wanted the *Herald* to rival the big-city newspapers of the east, and to date the *Herald* was sold in three neighboring counties, as well, with a growing circulation.

Tom looked up from his work to offer her a friendly smile. "Not at all, Tess. It's good to see you." He rose from his desk and they embraced briefly. "What brings you into town today?"

"Oh, I thought I'd visit Laura later today. But, actually, I came to see you first."

He pulled out a chair across from his desk. In the background she heard the sounds of the printing press and other workers conversing beyond the writing desk.

"Please sit down."

"Thank you."

Tom waited until she took her seat before he sat again. Tess always felt that Tom and Laura were the perfect match for one another. He was taller than most men, a little leaner, too. He had a kind face and a witty mind and he loved Laura to distraction. Seeing him today was a refreshing change from the kind of man she'd been subjected to lately. Certainly Tom and Clint had very little in common, except they were both dogged in their endeavors, Tom's being far more altruistic.

"How is Laura feeling lately?"

"She's doing fine. Just fine. We're expecting the little one any day now."

"I'm thrilled for you both."

Tom ran his hand through his hair nervously. "It's hard to believe we'll be parents soon. It's what Laura and I have wanted for quite some time now."

"It's a precious gift." When Tess looked at Tom, she hadn't realized she'd given away her innermost feelings until she saw the sympathetic expression on his face.

"It'll happen for you one day, Tess."

"I'm a widow with no plans to marry again, so it's doubtful." Then she turned her attention to the real reason for her visit. "I came here to ask you a favor, Tom. I'm planning on having a women's meeting in town and I'd like you to print up the invitations for me."

He began nodding almost immediately, taking up

a pen to jot things down. "Do you want it to go into the *Herald*?"

"Yes, but I want small posters, as well, that I can distribute to all Hayworth holdings. I want the men to know I fully expect their wives and daughters to be present at this meeting. I've given it some thought. What do you think of Hayworth's Sociable Ladies Alliance Partnership? S-L-A-P."

Tom's attention riveted to her face, his eyes opening wider. "Is that what you honestly want me to write?"

Tess sighed. "If I thought I could get away with it, I'd say yes, because there's a bit of the devil in me. I want to make my point, but I need to be more discreet than that. There's no telling how far I can push—but, darn it, this is important, and I want the women to open up and have the freedoms I never had."

"Not SLAP, then," Tom said with relief. "This is about those women you and Laura have been seeing, isn't it?"

"Yes, it is. It's time someone stood up for women who haven't found a way to stand up for themselves yet. It's time they learned that they don't have to take the mistreatment they've been handed. If I have to use the Hayworth name and resources to help them, then I will with an open heart."

Tom began nodding again. "So what will you call these mandatory meetings?"

"Oh, I'm sure we'll find a gentler way to term it, Tom. The meetings aren't by any means obligatory, but you'll be sure to note in your invitation that I'd be greatly disappointed if some of the women couldn't attend. *Understood?*"

He set down his pen and rubbed at the morning stubble on his jaw. "Understood, Tess. Bullying the menfolk, aren't you?"

"Just playing the cards in my hand."

"With a stacked deck?" His thin brows rose in question, but his smile held approval.

"But I'm not bluffing. Hoyt helped me and I'm going to do my best to help other women. I'll use the Hayworth influence for some good."

"I admire you and what you're trying to do, but I'm not entirely sure—"

"I know what I'm facing, Tom. I know that some men won't be agreeable, but I'm holding the winning cards and I need to help." Then a notion filtered in and she smiled with satisfaction. "Why, that's the perfect name, don't you agree?"

"What is?" His brows gathered in confusion now.

"Hayworth's Exceptional Ladies Partnership— striving for excellence…in womanhood."

Tom's eyes lit with amusement. "H-E-L-P."

"Exactly."

They both nodded at the same time.

Tom picked up his pen again. "Now just fill me in on the details. When? Where? Topics of discussion?"

Twenty minutes later Tess walked out of Tom's office feeling better than she had since before Hoyt's death almost four months ago.

* * *

Laura looked well, though heavy with child and tiring easily. Tess kept her visit short, understanding her friend needed rest, and returned to the ranch late in the afternoon. She pulled the buggy up to the stables, and young Randy Wilcott came over to help her down, his gaze and attention directed toward the corral.

"Ain't he a beauty, Mrs. Hayworth?"

She turned in that direction and saw a magnificent palomino, racing up and back, frantically searching for a way out, his lush white mane flowing, his coat shining like a gold coin in the afternoon sunlight. She recalled Hoyt's obsession with catching this wild horse. He'd had a corral built higher than most with one added rung of fencing to keep the elusive palomino from making the jump—if ever they'd managed to catch the stallion.

"They finally got him," she marveled, her voice drifting. She watched the horse fight for his freedom, snorting and huffing out breaths.

Hoyt would have been pleased seeing the palomino on his land, in his corral. He'd held a fascination for the stallion, spotting him on his land in his healthier days and wanting that steed for himself. When she'd questioned the justice of penning an animal who longed to be free, Hoyt had assured her, "No need to worry. He's an untamed spirit, Tess. He'll always be free." His eyes had glittered at the prospect.

"Mr. Hayworth plans on riding him one day,"

Randy said with exuberance. "The boys are taking bets how many times he gets thrown. I got me a bet on thirty times."

Tess glanced at Randy, and her good mood soured when the palomino rose up, his forelegs lifting in a fit of frustration. "He'll get trampled."

"We've got us bets on that, too," he said before catching himself. "Oh, I mean, not that we want that to happen. And if anybody can take the vinegar outta that horse, it'd be Mr. Hayworth. He's got him a knack, he does. We've all seen it, ma'am."

Tess had seen it, too, but she feared Clint had met his match. The palomino wasn't just wild; this horse seemed borne of the land, as ferocious as Texas storms and as powerful as a rushing river. There was something in his coal black eyes that put fear in her. And once again she marveled at how she could find such beauty in something so innately fierce.

Clint came out of the bunkhouse, laughing with one of the ranch hands, and strode up to the fence. Wearing his hat, he tied leather chaps over his trousers, his gaze directly on the stallion.

"Excuse me, Randy." Tess lifted her skirts and walked over to the corral fence to stand beside Clint. "You're not going to try to tame him?"

Clint stared ahead, watching every move the animal made. "I'm thinking on it."

"Well, think again. He'll crush you."

Clint grinned and turned to her. "I'm touched that you care."

The teasing tone in his voice only added to her exasperation. She couldn't stand by and see Hoyt's only son injured or killed. "You may think me heartless, but I do care. I wouldn't want to see anyone injured on this ranch."

"*Anyone?* Or *me?*" he said quietly, watching her with close scrutiny.

Tess's heart sped. Something was happening to her. She didn't welcome the feelings and she fought them hard, but she couldn't deny that when Clint looked at her she reacted with a strange kind of desire.

She'd had to lie most of her adult life about her situation, but she wasn't good at lying about her *feelings.* Those were raw and honest, and when Clint looked into her eyes she couldn't conceal them. As crazy as that was, since he was by law her stepson, her adversary and her biggest hindrance on the ranch, she knew that Clint Hayworth could have a big impact on her life.

She was sure that wasn't a good thing, but nonetheless the certainty of it made her breath catch in her throat. "What if I told you, I'm not sure?"

Clint's dark brows lifted an increment. "Then I'd say I admire your honesty."

"Well, that's a start. I didn't think you admired anything about me."

He laughed, raking over her body in a hot gaze, grazing her breasts, then lifting to her mouth. "Then you'd be dead wrong."

A shot of heat scurried up and down her body.

Clint made her nerves quiver. "You haven't called me a whore in a few days—I suppose that's progress," she said in a rush, then immediately wished she could take those words back.

Clint took his Stetson off, ran a hand through his hair, then reset the hat atop his head. "Well, now, if you're attempting to distract me, you're doing a good job."

Clint had a way of misinterpreting her meaning. She decided a change of subject was needed. She couldn't take the intensity of his stare much longer. "Clint, do you know what your father said about the palomino?"

"I don't care to know."

She ignored him. "He said a fiery spirit like the palomino's would always be free. There's no sense trying to tame him, Clint."

"Yet Hoyt wanted the stallion, right? He put out an order to the men, offering a reward for the man who brought him in, because the palomino poised a challenge. He wanted what he couldn't have. He wanted that stallion to lord over and for no other reason."

"That's not true."

Clint watched the stallion prance haughtily over the earth, caged and ready to break free if given the chance. "It is, Tess. Wake up. See the man for who he was."

There was no use arguing with him about Hoyt. "So why don't *you* set him free? You could do it. Open the gate and let him go."

"Don't compare me to my father. We're nothing

alike. My intentions toward that animal have nothing to do with wanting to possess it."

Confused and filled with rising frustration, Tess shook her head. "Then why, Clint? Why would you attempt to tame that horse?"

"To save it," he said plain and simple. Then he shot her a look. "There are other things I want to possess."

She took a swallow. "The ranch?"

He laughed again, quietly. "Meet me out here late tonight and I'll answer that question." He turned and walked away.

Tess watched him go, her heart in her throat. His invitation thrilled her, the excitement soaring through her system like an eagle in flight. But she was relieved at the same time. At least for today she'd succeeded in keeping Clint out of that corral and out of danger.

But he was a Hayworth.

And Hayworth men always achieved what they set out to do, regardless of the consequences.

Chapter Seven

Tess sat at the kitchen table eating her evening meal in silence. Greta fussed over her, setting dishes of spiced beef, creamy potatoes, beets and string beans in front of her. The cook hadn't come around, leastwise not that Tess could tell, but a dose of pride and a strong work code had her fixing up plates of food and serving her fare as if Tess were royalty. No one would ever best Greta Deutch.

So as not to upset the cook, Tess put small amounts of food on her plate and began nibbling. She had little appetite tonight.

"Wouldt be better if Clint ate here each night."

Most nights he chose to eat outdoors with the ranch hands. Greta spent her days cooking the morning and evening meals to send out to the men. Hoyt had insisted they eat well, and Greta took great pride in the ranch hands' meals, as well. Randy and another man would come in and take the big pots of food out to the men, and occasionally Greta would go outside to serve them and make sure they had enough to eat, but secretly Tess believed she enjoyed receiving their compliments and praise.

"Clint doesn't like the company in here," Tess replied, gaining a grunt from Greta.

"He's a *goodt* man. He *needts* a *goodt* woman."

And that didn't mean her, the money-grubbing, deceitful woman who'd come to the ranch looking for employment and managed to marry Greta's employer, the richest man in the territory. Her message came through clearly.

"I know you miss Clint, Greta. Maybe if I ate my meals in my room, he'd eat inside more."

Greta put one hand on Tess's shoulder, keeping her in her seat. "You sit. Your place is here."

Tess looked up from the table to meet with Greta's light brown eyes. Greta nodded for an instant, then made herself busy with pouring coffee into a gold-edged china cup decorated with roses.

Tess smiled inwardly. She'd hoped Greta would come around and maybe this was her first gesture of acceptance. Hoyt wouldn't stand for anything but her full approval, so Greta had been civil to Tess while Hoyt was alive, but afterward Greta had looked upon her as a trespasser. She didn't trust her, believing, like Clint, that she was out to usurp the family fortune and good name.

Tess cleared away her plate, meeting with a quick

but gentle slap on the hand from Greta, who immediately took the plate from her.

Tess flinched from the contact, jumping back in-
stinctively, recalling her father's brutal touch.

*Take this damn plate away. Lousy imitation of a
meal anyway.*

She shook off the harsh reminder of her childhood.

"*Goodt*ness." Greta appeared momentarily shaken.
"You *godt* to be strong."

"I'm trying, Greta."

Her comment came out sounding like a weary,
defeated plea, and Greta's expression changed. She
turned knowing eyes her way. "You don't let any
man *hurdt* you ever again."

Was it that obvious? Tess thought she'd been
doing a good job of hiding her secrets and her past.
But the truth remained that men had hurt her, both
physically and emotionally. And she struggled every
day to be strong, to be free of that confining prison.
Most days she succeeded, and nothing surprised her
more than her recoil at Greta's light but revealing re-
primand just now.

"I don't plan to, Greta. Sometimes it's hard forgetting."

Greta closed her eyes. "I know."

"You do?"

She nodded and looked at Tess with newfound
understanding. "I left my *husbandt* many years ago. He
was not kind. He is dead now. And it's a *goodt* thing."

"Oh, Greta, I'm sorry."

Greta set her lips in a smile so rare and heart-warming that Tess could have hugged her. "My sorrow was over long ago, but the memories stay if you let them. You *shouldt* let them go."

"Oh, Greta," she said with a measure of hope now. "I will let them go…in time."

And then Tess revealed her plan to help the women of Hâyworth who would otherwise have nowhere else to turn for help, explaining about the meetings with that very same name. In those moments, something shifted slightly in the universe between her and Greta. Through a mutual history they seemed to have formed a tentative bond.

When Tess left the kitchen, she climbed the stairs to her bedroom feeling exhausted both mentally and physically. Her bed beckoned, the comfort of a soft mattress and even softer goose-feather pillows.

She undressed slowly, removing her shoes and stockings and her gown, putting everything away neatly. She moved to the window to take one last look at the land and wish Hoyt a goodnight, as she had every night since he'd died, the ritual beginning when he'd taken very ill.

"What's it look like tonight?" he'd ask from his bed. "Tell me, how many stars are out? Has peace settled over the ranch yet?"

And Tess would tell him when he was too weak to see for himself. After his death she continued in that practice, appraising the land, the stars and the

ranch he loved so much, silently, her way of assuring
him she would carry out his last wishes.

A shadow of a man caught her eye. Out by the
palomino's corral. Surely it wasn't Clint.

Meet me out here late tonight.

Had he been serious with that taunt? The notion
had put exciting images in her head all day long, and
if truth be told, she'd secretly wanted to meet him.

There are others things I want to possess.

Her mind reeled. What would it be like to be possessed by Clint? Would he make good the promise
in his eyes?

She stared at the corral, and the man turned, as if
he'd known she was there. Dressed in her pale white
chemise, Tess knew she should draw the curtain and
move away from the window, but instead she stood
there as if she'd been planted into a deep, tight hole,
rooted with no way out.

Clint stood in the moon's shadow. The brim of
his hat shaded his face entirely, but then he pushed
his brim up higher on his forehead and he came into
full view. Even from this distance she witnessed
raw desire on face, his smile, unabashed and...
sinful.

Tess drew her hand to her chest, reacting to him,
the look of pure lust on his face and the desire bat-
tling within her. Her bones melting, she didn't know
what to do. The temptation pulled at her and she
fought it like a tug-of-war.

But her next move was decided undeniably when

Clint turned back around to the palomino's corral and climbed the rungs, jumping over the fence.

"Clint!" she called out, though she doubted he could hear her or if her alarm would matter to him one bit.

She put her robe on, slid her feet into slippers and raced down the stairs, out into the dark night.

"Are you crazy?" she whispered with a sharp intake of breath. She trained her gaze on the palomino at the far side of the corral. His nostrils flared. His breaths spurted out. He appeared ready to charge.

She kept her voice low, but the palomino barely noticed her, both man and animal locked down in a stare as Clint stood facing him from the opposite end of the corral.

"I'm marking my territory." Clint didn't move a muscle. "Letting him know I'm here."

"I'd say you've made your point," she said in a hushed tone. Clint was hard to miss; his presence dominated wherever he went.

"Not yet." He continued to stare.

Through the shadows of darkness the moon cast light on the horse's coat, making him appear a golden mythical beast that might fly off into the clouds at any moment.

Oh, if only.

Tess held her breath. Clint knew what he was doing. The set of his jaw and the determination on his face had to mean something.

"He's a smart one."

"He looks angry."

"He is. But he's frustrated, too. He's trapped and wants out."

Clint could have been speaking about himself. He'd never wanted to come back to the Double H. He'd trapped himself in this vendetta against his father.

"You understand him?"

Clint slid his gaze to hers. "I do."

The break in the stare-down riled the horse. He snorted with rising fury, then rushed forward, charging Clint.

To her amazement, Clint held his ground, keeping his gaze on the horse.

"Clint!"

Then, at the last possible second, Clint hurled himself over the fence, landing solidly on his heels.

The palomino stopped, stomped, snorted, then raced around the perimeter of the corral, thrusting himself side to side in a fury.

Clint took his hat off and slapped it to his knee, a big childlike grin on his face.

"You scared me half to death!" Tess was not amused—nor was she immune to his infectious smile.

"It's nothing to worry over, Tess. I've done this before."

"I'm not worried," she said in a full-out lie.

His smile grew wider. "I know what I'm doing."

She liked him better when he had a scowl on his face. At least that way she couldn't entertain thoughts of liking him. As it was now, she had to remind herself why he'd come back to the Double H and what his intentions were.

"Do you?" she asked.

"I got you to meet me out here tonight."

She opened her mouth. Then clamped it shut, taken aback by his clever maneuver.

The stallion simmered down, taking his place at the far end of the corral, watching them with cautious eyes, his snorts coming less frequently now.

Tess didn't have that same luxury. She couldn't simmer down. Her heart raced. Her body trembled. She'd been afraid for Clint's life. And now she stood outside in the dark but for a brilliant slice of moonlight, with stars shining overhead, seeing a look of triumph on his face.

"I saw you up in the window, Tess. You wanted me to look at you. So don't pretend shock that you're here with me now."

"You could have been trampled to death!"

"And you don't want anyone getting hurt on the ranch, right?"

Again Tess opened her mouth, but she shut it just as quickly. There wasn't any use sparring words with him. He'd just jumble them up to make them come out the way he wanted. "I'm going back inside."

She turned to leave and got three steps away when Clint sidled up next to her, taking her hand and tugging her toward the barn. Oddly his touch didn't send her into a panic. She followed him, and when they reached the barn, Clint whipped around to lean his back against the wall, drawing her to him and sliding his hands around her waist.

He held her carefully, without menace or threat, and she went willingly to him, allowing him the liberty of brushing her body to his, finding his gentle strength thrilling.

A half smile on his lips brought her attention to his mouth, and when she looked at him, he searched her face for a moment, their eyes locking.

Hidden against the dark side of the barn, where moonlight seemed to have vanished, Clint dropped his hands lower, his fingers splaying wide, making circles on the small of her back, sending magnificent shivers spiraling through her body. "You like the feel of that, honey?" His voice flowed out like smooth silk.

Tess swallowed and stood still, wanting his touch, but fearing it, too.

He moved his hands farther down, to the very tips of her derriere, stirring her senses and creating havoc inside. Her breaths came rapidly and her emotions rocked out of control.

"You know what I want to do." Silk again, smooth and edged with promise.

"Clint," she said, meant as a warning, but his name came out a breathless whisper.

He smiled right before he cupped her head with one hand and drew her lips to his. Their mouths mated and she reeled from the initial contact. Every nerve ending tingled with pleasure.

Sure and confidently, he moved his mouth over

hers, but with enough gentleness to assure her freedom. It was her decision to make, but ultimately it was not. She couldn't deny the impact of his kiss or the flutters inside from being claimed by this man.

He stroked her lips with the tip of his tongue, outlining their shape, then plunged deeper into her mouth, until small pleasured sounds escaped her throat. Their tongues mated, causing rapid-fire heat to shoot through to her woman's center. A tiny ache built between her legs, and she felt unfulfilled and needy, a sensation altogether new to Tess.

She cupped Clint's face now, responding to his passion and stroking him the way he did her, returning his kisses with equal enthusiasm.

He held her firmly and she arched her back, allowing him access to her throat. He drizzled kisses there, wetting her skin and catching the coolness of the outside air.

Her senses spiraling out of control, she barely felt the sash to her robe coming undone. It hung now from her shoulders, exposing her chemise. "I've seen you without this robe, Tess. I want to see you again."

She squeezed her eyes shut, but when she reopened them Clint's eyes were on her, his hot gaze ready to devour her.

He touched the skin just above the lace of her chemise, his fingers teasing the valley between her breasts until she nearly cried out for more. He witnessed her desire and drew a deep breath, then thumbed one nipple, flicking the tip until it puckered up from under the material. She flinched, and that ache between her legs intensified with hot, fiery waves, her want undeniable.

Her breaths came rapidly now, her heart pounding.

"Lay with me," he whispered. "I'll show you what it's like to be with a real man."

For a moment she wanted nothing more but to lay with him. To give in to him. To let him take her. But his words stopped her cold. She took a good long look into his gleaming eyes before she removed his hand from her breast and retied the sash to her robe.

Clint didn't really want her. He wanted to best his father—to show Hoyt up and lay claim to his widow. The cool splash of reality brought her to her senses. She stepped away from him. "I've known a real man, Clint."

He stared at her, his lips quirking up. "Don't be a fool, Tess."

Her lips burned for his kiss and every bone in her body ached for his touch. Yet, there wasn't anything *real* about Clint.

He was a deceiver and a vengeful man.

She smiled with great remorse. "I almost was a fool...*just now.*"

Clint watched her leave, her head held high, her body straight, but the slight tremble in her strides told him what he needed to know.

He spun around and headed back to the corral, shaking off sensations that rippled through him like a forceful downriver stream.

For a minute Tess had made him forget she was his father's widow. He'd almost forgotten his purpose in coming back to the ranch. But he wouldn't soon forget holding her in his arms and kissing her. He wouldn't forget the liberties she'd granted him or his instant arousal when he'd touched her skin and fondled her breasts, making her breaths catch and her body melt.

Leaning against the fence post, he focused instead on the stallion, who had settled down, unaware of Clint's presence. He'd never come up against an animal with such a strong will. Clint's gift for bringing animals into his circle of trust seemed nonexistent with this one stallion. But he wouldn't give up.

The golden animal he'd named Sunset wouldn't best him.

They'd come to an understanding soon.

The twitch in his pants reminded him of another stubborn creature. Only he had no plans to tame Tess.

No, he wanted her wild and wanton.

Both horse and woman posed a challenge, and he wouldn't cease until he'd achieved his goals.

Shortly after, Clint went inside and climbed the stairs. He entered the hallway, the house and surroundings quiet but for the sound of his boots scraping against the wooden floors.

He still tasted Tess's sweetened breath on his mouth, and her fragrant scent lingered in his nostrils. He'd pulled her against the barn, and she'd gone willingly, flowing into him from his slightest tug.

Her body had pressed to his and sparked quick, hot desire. That desire hadn't waned or ebbed but rather embedded within him.

He stopped outside her door. Put his hand on her doorknob. Listened.

The silence in her room irked him.

She slept.

She would lay with him one night—he would make sure of it. But it wouldn't be tonight.

He continued down the hallway and entered his room. He set his hat on a hook, sat on his bed, ready to remove his boots, when a flash of light caught his eye. He turned fully to look out his window.

"Dammit!"

He grabbed his hat and raced down the stairs to the bunkhouse. He pounded on the door, shouting and hoping to wake every able-bodied man. "Fire! Out by the storage shed. Move! Now!"

Clint didn't wait for the men to rouse. He mounted a horse and rode bareback to the shed that sat on the outlying area of the ranch grounds. There wasn't much he could do but kick dirt onto flames shooting skyward, the roof fully engulfed and ready to collapse.

When the men arrived with buckets, they set up a water line that led from the water tank to the fire. They worked together for the better part of an hour, dousing bucket after bucket on the shed, splashing water out in their haste to contain the flames.

Clint stood in the front lines, gripping the buckets,

heaving water and hoping to stop the fire before it caused too much destruction. One of the men gave him a bandanna to cover his face, and all men followed suit, trying to keep their lungs clear while they squinted their eyes fighting against the stinging smoke.

He figured the shed and all its contents—wheat, oats, barley, straw and various ranch tools—were destroyed, but he couldn't let the fire jump.

They continued to douse water into the night until all that was left of the shed were molten ashes, steaming with heat and smoke.

Sometime during the chaos Tess had appeared, dressed in her tan riding pants and boots. She'd worked the back of the line with the men, filling buckets and handing them off. Her face soot-stained, her hair in a tangle, she walked over to him as they both surveyed the damage. Smoke billowed up, bathing their faces in dirty steam.

"We'll need to get more feed in town for the livestock. We'll rebuild."

Clint looked at her. Heard the determination in her voice.

"There's another shed on the property," he said.

She shook her head. "It's not big enough. But it'll have to do for now. When Sonny gets here, have him send a man into town for supplies."

"Already done."

She nodded. "I don't suppose anyone saw anything?"

"Nope. They were all sleeping when I spotted the flames."

"*You* discovered the fire?"

He drew oxygen into his lungs. He didn't like the accusation in her tone or the way she searched his face. "I came inside a while after you did. Wasn't more than two minutes before I saw the shed go up."

She used her shirtsleeve to wipe sweat from her brow and move strands of hair from her eyes as she continued to watch him.

"I suppose it's a good thing you saw the fire when you did," she said with enough reluctance to irritate him. Then she turned to the men and got their attention by raising her voice. "Thank you, all. You've worked hard tonight. Go back to bed and take the morning for yourselves."

"There's work to do in the morning," Clint said to her, peeved that she'd taken it upon herself to give the men time off. Seems they were coming around and starting to respect their lady boss.

"It can wait."

Clint ground his teeth.

"What can't wait is finding out who's doing this."

Clint agreed with that. "That's why we're setting up guards around the ranch. I don't care what Sonny thinks. Things could have gotten outta hand tonight if I hadn't seen those flames when I did."

Tess arched her brows but said nothing.

But Clint knew her suspicions, and they were directed solely at him. "You've got it dead wrong, Tess."

"Do I?" she asked, perplexed, looking at him for answers.

Hell, he had no answers. He shrugged. "Believe what you want, I'm not here to prove anything to anyone. You know why I came."

"Is that the only reason you're staying?"

"Damn right it is," Clint said, nodding his head. He wouldn't show Tess the inkling of doubt creeping into his mind about the Double H. "Come on," he said, taking her arm and leading her away from the burned shed. "We can't do anything more here tonight."

"No," she whispered, and he didn't miss the irony of her next words. "We've done quite enough."

Chapter Eight

Early in the morning Clint stood by the downed shed, the acrid smell of destruction filling his nostrils and mixed with an eerily familiar scent wafting through the air of burned oatmeal. He picked up a shovel and dashed the last remaining embers with dirt, more to occupy his hands than any concern over those few hot spots that were dying out on their own.

He'd slept restlessly last night, scouring his mind for the reasons behind these incidents at the ranch. And when sleep had eluded him, impatient, he'd risen from bed before dawn and come outside to think.

He didn't like being threatened. He wasn't a man to stand by and watch his property abused like this. For the time being anyway, the Double H was his ranch. He'd come to know the men—all good men who'd served Hoyt with loyalty. And now they took orders from his widow, some with grudging respect and others out of duty. She signed off to them on payday, after all.

But he was amazed at Tess. She'd dug right in last night and worked hard, helping douse the flames. She'd lined up with the crew as if one of them and hadn't stopped to rest or complain. She was no wilting flower. He'd seen her lift those buckets and move them along the line as ably as any man, though there'd been strain on her face and worry in her eyes.

She'd made plans to rebuild and given orders without hesitation or doubt.

Out of his resentment, a measure of unwanted admiration took hold in his gut. He didn't want it. It was as unwelcome as the taste of soured milk.

But he did want her.

Plain fact: she tempted him with those summer-sky eyes well versed in concealing her truths. He recognized it every time he looked at himself in a mirror, seeing the death of innocence on his own face. He knew that secrets Tess had locked away in her soul had followed her to the Double H.

They had that in common.

When he'd touched her skin, so fine and smooth and polished, she'd welcomed him. He'd been easy with her, caressing her with tenderness born of deep desire, knowing that's what she'd needed. But it hadn't been easy to hold back, to restrain what wanted unleashing inside him.

One day she would give herself freely to him—and he would take her.

And he wouldn't concern himself with anything but bringing them both a good deal of pleasure. Her troubles were hers alone. Clint couldn't afford to care.

That was not his purpose.

Sonny's gruff voice from behind stopped him from shoveling the next clump of dirt. "I guess I missed the excitement last night. Had me a good night's sleep. Should have sent one of the boys to wake me."

Clint planted his shovel in the earth and leaned onto it. "Couldn't spare a man to fetch you. The flames went up quick-like. It was a good thing I spotted them straightaway."

Sonny nodded and eyed the damage without flinching or bringing accusation to his expression.

"We lost the shed and all its contents—but they're replaceable. We'll rebuild. We sent two men into town to get the supplies we need," Clint said.

"The whole ranch could've gone up if the flames went without notice." Sonny slapped his shoulder. "You did good, Clint."

"Gut reactions, Sonny. If those flames had jumped, the barn could've been next…or the bunkhouse."

"You saved lives last night, boy." The admiration in his tone unwound a tight coil inside. Sonny had always been a source of support and friendship, and Clint had forgotten what that felt like. His praise meant something.

"I'm just glad I spotted it when I did."

"Did Mrs. Hayworth see the damage yet?"

"She was out here last night, working the fire lines."

"You don't say? She's got a spark in her, that woman."

Clint held back a comment. He'd seen her spark. She'd practically ignited in his arms last night, and he'd not soon forget how that felt.

"Soon as the embers cool completely, have a few men clear the area."

"Will do. We'll get a new shed built by tomorrow's end."

Still baffled by these incidents of sabotage, he drew sooty air deep into his lungs. "What's your take on all this, Sonny? Who do you suppose is doing this? And why? There's potential danger, but the acts themselves cause more nuisance than anything else."

"I know. I don't understand it myself." Sonny moved away from the smoke that seemed to be bothering his eyes.

Clint felt the sting, too, after standing over the ashes, pitching dirt. "There's got to be a reason."

"Don't know one," he said, shaking his head.

"We're putting guards up around the ranch. There's no choice now."

Sonny let go a resigned breath. "I suppose you got a point."

"Damn right I do. So far no one's been hurt, and I intend to keep it that way."

"Don't sound like a man bent on revenge anymore, Clint."

"Don't mistake my concern for human and animal

lives for any love I have for the ranch. They're two different things, Sonny."

Sonny removed his hat to scratch his head. His eyes narrowed to a squint. "Guards, huh?"

Clint assured him with a nod. "The boys will take turns, won't be so hard on them. And tell them they'll get more than a day's extra pay for each shift they work. There's a big bonus if they catch the ones responsible for this. You tell them that, too."

Again Sonny scratched his head. "Mrs. Hayworth okay with this?"

Clint cocked his lips to one side. "She has no choice. This is how it's gonna be."

One week after the fire at the ranch Tess paid a visit to Laura. She'd always loved Tom and Laura's small, charming house that bordered the east side of town. Theirs was a real home, especially now that they were a family.

"You don't have to wait on me, Tess," Laura said quietly, looking up from the bundle in her arms.

Tess poured steaming tea into patterned china cups and set them down on the parlor table. She watched new mother and baby with envious eyes, her insides softening to butter. She spoke in softened tones so as not to wake the baby. "You're right. I'm not about to let you hold little Miss Abigail Larson without sharing."

Tess leaned down and took the babe from Laura's giving arms. "Come here to your Aunt Tess, Abby.

We'll let your mama drink her tea. You gave her a tough time coming out and now she needs her rest."

As soon as Abby was safely ensconced, Laura leaned back in the sofa seat and sighed wearily. "She's worth all the trouble."

Tess sat beside her carefully, arranging the blanket and looking into the sleeping face of the most beautiful baby she'd ever seen. "She's precious, Laura. You're so fortunate."

"I know. Tom and I feel blessed. It's just that I'm…tired all the time."

"I suppose that's natural. You had the pains for nearly a full day. It wasn't an easy delivery."

Laura's gaze fell on her child. "No, not easy, but she's perfect. I'm grateful for that."

"She is. But you're not. You could use a little break, Laura. I see how tired you are, even while you try to hide it from me. I'd like to stay over tonight to help out."

"Tess, I'm…fine. You don't have to."

"I *want* to." She gazed down at the week-old child in her arms and rocked her gently. There was such beauty and innocence in a new life. Such hope. "Besides, I need to make further arrangements for HELP tomorrow. The first meeting is next week. I hope you'll be feeling well enough to come."

"I'll be there, Tess. I wouldn't want to miss that."

"Good, then let me tend to Abby today and tonight while you get back into bed and get some sleep."

"But Tom will need supper when he gets home and—"

"I'll take care of Tom and the baby. Please, Laura, let me do this for you. I'll leave in the morning."

"You'll bring Abby in when she's hungry?"

Tess smiled. "Of course." She glanced quickly to her own breasts, then grinned even more. "That's one way I *can't* help you."

They both chuckled.

"Thank you."

"You're welcome. Please, have your tea and then settle into bed while Abby and I get better acquainted. And don't worry about a thing."

Tess spent the rest of the day tending to little Abigail Larson. While the baby slept, she looked in on Laura. And when the child wakened, needing a change of clothing, Tess relished every second of cleaning and redressing her and rocking her back to sleep. She'd brought Abby in to Laura twice during the day to nurse until both mother and baby fell into slumber again.

Often Abby's breaths would come fast, in quick bursts, then she'd quiet down for a long few seconds when it appeared she wasn't breathing at all. Laura told her it's the way with new babies—they are just learning to fill their lungs, and their irregular breathing was enough to keep a new mama up all night watching them.

While thick soup boiled on the cookstove and ebbing sunshine gave way to dusky afternoon shadows, tears glistened in Tess's eyes as she watched the baby in her arms now. She'd never know this joy for herself. She'd never have a baby of her own. Tess had long ago given up on the dream that so many women took for granted.

She wanted a family. She wanted tenderness and innocence brought back into her life. She yearned for someone to love, someone to give her children, but deep down Theresa Metcalf knew she wouldn't attain that dream. Thanks to Hoyt, she no longer believed that she didn't deserve those things. But she doubted she'd ever get the chance. She had other obligations now, other heartfelt duties to perform.

She didn't trust easily. There were only a few people in her life she called "friend." And now she had little Abby to adore. She would love this child as if it were her own. She already did love her. But Abby had a wonderful mother and father.

Tess would be the outsider again.

She'd fight those feelings embedded in her because she knew Tom and Laura loved her and did everything in their power to make her feel welcome.

A sole tear escaped the well she'd tried to shore up. It trickled down her face and dropped onto the baby's fat cheek. Abby opened her eyes and looked straight up at her, those blue, blue eyes so clear, watching her.

Tess smiled at the baby she held. "You are so blessed. You have two parents who treasure you, Abby. And an aunt who will always be here for you."

Then she sobbed quietly, both with joy over this new life and with sorrow, her heart hurting for the child Tess would never have of her own.

* * *

"The posters are perfect, Tom. Thank you. I plan to distribute them tomorrow," Tess said, sitting across from him in the parlor.

Tom held little Abby in his arms, watching her with a look of pride and awe. Reluctantly he tore his gaze away from his daughter to look at Tess. "I hope it works. I won't tell you what the men at the *Herald* said when I was printing them up."

Tess frowned but wouldn't be dissuaded. She held the posters in her hand, perusing them with satisfaction. Tom had done exactly as she'd asked, making the posters look like delicate invitations to her first women's meeting.

Hayworth's Exceptional Ladies Partnership.

Everyone in attendance would receive a special gift from Mrs. Hayworth and the Double H ranch.

"I suppose they aren't happy."

"Not exactly. They don't understand why you need a woman's meeting in the middle of the week. Takes the women away from their chores." The baby fussed and he rocked her gently until she quieted. "I can imagine what they'd say if they knew your true intent."

"Most are good, decent men, Tom. But some are…not so decent."

"It's a good thing you're doing, Tess," he said with a quick smile. "Just hope it works."

Tess nodded. "So do I."

"Thank you for helping out with Laura today. She's pretending otherwise, but I know she's exhausted."

"She didn't fool me, either. She's sleeping soundly. I won't wake her for supper. I made you a meal and we can have that as soon as you'd like."

"You're a good friend, Tess. As soon as Abby falls back asleep, let's have that soup. Smells darn good."

Thirty minutes later they'd filled their bellies. Tom insisted on cleaning up the dishes, and they worked for a few minutes in companionable silence until the dishes were dried and stacked away.

"I heard about the fire out at the ranch," he said, returning to the table with two mugs of coffee. He slid one toward her place at the table and gestured for her to sit.

"How did you hear about that?" She dried her hands on a kitchen cloth and took a seat.

Tom blew into his cup, cooling down his coffee. "Hayworth news travels fast. Randy came into town, buying up new supplies."

"We're being sabotaged. Both Clint and Sonny are in agreement now. Clint set up guards to work in shifts around the ranch." Tess sighed wearily. "I just don't know who would do this or…why."

"Hoyt wasn't a man who enjoyed making enemies, but I suppose there's some out there who didn't like his business tactics. He's gone…so who would stand to gain anything by doing this now?"

Tess bit her lip, then shared her suspicions with Tom. "There's…Clint."

"Clint? You don't really think he's behind all this?"

She shook her head and sipped her coffee, contemplating. "I don't know. He makes no secret that he wants to buy me out of my half of the ranch. Scaring me and making things difficult to run the ranch might be his way of helping that along. And yet he's the first one to fix whatever problems crop up from the sabotage. It's a mystery. And it's strange to think someone's out there, planning on hurting the Double H." The notion brought prickly bumps to her arms. Made her quiver with trepidation.

"Be careful, Tess." He sipped coffee again. "Laura and I think of you as family."

"I'm careful." She'd been cautious for all her years. She always looked over her shoulder and protected herself because no one had ever cared enough to do it for her except for her dear friends. "And I think of you as family, too," she managed, refusing to get emotional again, though a swell of love coursed through her from his kind words.

The baby fussed with the sweetest cries and small movements that said she needed nourishment. "Do you want to take her in to Laura? Or shall I?" she asked.

"You sit, Tess. Relax some. I'll take her in to see her mama."

"Laura will be happy to see you tonight."

"I hope she got the rest she needed."

"I think she did. Give her a few days, Tom. She'll be herself again soon."

Tom left the room with a worried expression, and Tess only marveled at how much he loved his wife, how close they were and how now they had a little one to bond that love even more.

Tess walked outside to a sultry night, the air heavy and thick. She sat on a bench seat on the ▼ porch and gazed at the stars as loneliness seeped into her soul. The desolate feeling always hovered nearby, ready to take control. She'd been its victim of her life. Only meeting Hoyt had changed that, those few months the lonely feelings had peared. But Hoyt was gone now and Tess had ferent life.

She didn't want to go back to that insecu hesitant, uneasy woman she once was. But at th moment, thinking of her dear friends and their new baby, sharing the wonderful newness of family, Tess had never felt more alone.

Her mind drifted to Clint.

And for the first time she realized how much they had in common. Both were fighting past hurts. Both had been scarred by events out of their control.

She remembered how she'd felt when he'd held her sinfully close to him. When his lips had touched hers. The spark. The immediate connection. Sensations had ripped through her, robbing her breath, pumping her heart, making her feel safe even in his dangerous embrace.

In those moments she hadn't been lonely. In those moments she'd felt as if she belonged. She'd ached inside for wanting Clint to be any other man than the one bent on destroying his father's legacy.

She took another look skyward, noting the vastness of the night, and gave in to the loneliness she'd fought so valiantly for so long. Just for tonight, she allowed herself the freedom of surrender.

She entered Tom and Laura's home and settled in for the night, hoping sleep would claim her quickly.

Tomorrow, she had a mission to accomplish.

Tomorrow, she wouldn't be lonely.

Tess returned to the Double H the next afternoon, pulling her buggy up to the barn. She'd had a good day, leaving a well-rested Laura in better spirits, posting up her signs in town, speaking with her employees and hand-delivering some invitations to the homesteads on her way home. She'd set the meeting for Wednesday in the Hayworth Hotel's dining room.

Though the men she'd addressed seemed a bit confused when she'd spoken about her meeting, they'd agreed to give their wives, daughters or sisters the special invitation. She'd thought of doing this for so long and had hoped for a chance to meet with the women and speak from her heart. Now she'd be given the chance.

"You getting down from there or you gonna continue to daydream?"

Clint stood by the buggy's brake, and when she came out of her momentary haze, he smiled.

"Oh, uh, of course."

That rare smile did things to her. She had no call

thinking about him or how the deep sound of his voice stirred her senses.

He reached to help her down. She couldn't very well refuse. It was a polite gesture any man on the ranch would offer. But Clint wasn't just any man, and as soon as she set her hands on his shoulders and felt him gripping her waist, a rapid pulse beat in her throat as she recalled his kiss and the lusty way he'd touched her the other night.

She leaned into him and her breasts met with his chest. He let her down slowly, bracing her tight, their bodies brushing together as he lowered her. His scent of earth and work and man stirred her senses. She was drawn to him in an uncanny way and had no resistance when he held her so close.

When she stood on solid ground, his gaze locked to hers. "Enjoy your evening last night?"

Her breaths came fast. "Why? Did you miss me?" Nerves jangling, her jest had come out as a serious question, and heat rushed up her throat. Instant mortification set in.

He arched a brow while holding her to him. His gaze drifted to her mouth. "Maybe."

Her heart tripped over itself. It wasn't the response she'd expected from him. He continued to hold her around the waist and she continued to allow him. The connection strong, Tess had trouble thinking her next thought while his fingers applied slight, mesmerizing pressure to her waist. She fought female urges and remembered that they weren't alone. Ranch hands worked the property and could be looking on. "Let me be, Clint."

His lips quirked up naturally. "I don't have a hold on you, Tess."

When she looked down she discovered that, sure enough, Clint had released his hands from her waist. His touch had marked her somehow, and the lasting effect remained even after he'd physically let her go. Did he have another kind of hold on her? she wondered. One that couldn't be so easily broken?

Tess put her head down and sighed from the confounding thoughts swirling through her mind.

"Hard to believe little Laura is a mother now," he said.

Grateful the moment had passed, she nodded, sharing the same sentiment. She and Laura had always played house together. They'd always had dreams of a family. Now Laura's dream had come true. "She's exhausted but so happy. The baby is… glorious."

Clint stared at her, searching her eyes with a bit of puzzlement. "Don't tell me you're the motherly kind, Tess."

His doubts mingled with her misgivings and brought heaviness to her heart. She'd never really known her mother. She hadn't known guidance and faith and patience that came from a mother's love. She hadn't been taught the finer points of womanhood. She'd been raised by a man who had belittled her constantly, making her feel ugly and stupid and unloved.

She'd had an unholy family life. And when she'd grown older, she'd shot and killed her outlaw brother.

She often questioned what kind of mother she would make.

"No," she said finally. "No, I'm not the motherly kind."

Clint nodded. He seemed satisfied with her answer, as if she'd just affirmed his believed perception of her. The sting wounded her, and it was the kind of hurt that she couldn't speak. Yet the pain wedged deep within.

She turned from Clint and made a move toward the house, but he grabbed her hand, and she whirled around.

"I need to talk to you," he said, releasing her hand once he had her attention.

The unforgiving summer sun had blazed down all afternoon, making her wish for a cool drink and a refreshing bath. Anxious to get inside, away from Clint's probing eyes, she shook her head. "Can't it wait?"

He drew a long breath. "Don't think so. It's important."

"Meet me inside in a few minutes."

"No, we need to talk in private. Can't afford anyone to hear what I have to say."

Private? Then it dawned on her. "Did you find out something I should know about?"

"Maybe."

She heaved another sigh. Clint never gave an inch. She was forever trying to figure him out. "Where do you want to hold this private meeting?"

"Ride out to the creek with me."

The creek? Cool, shaded waters hidden between ancient oaks. The thought did appeal. The heat of the day had managed to stick her clothes to her skin.

"I'll saddle up the horses. Meet me here in twenty minutes."

The pull of refreshing waters and Clint's ominous meeting had her agreeing. She dashed into the house, climbing the stairs to her room. She undressed quickly, peeling away her sweat-stained dress, and bathed her skin in rose-scented water. The air inside her room stifled despite the lateness of the afternoon and the open window. Tess had learned to adjust to Texas heat, though she often thought of the cool northern California days that were fresh and crisp and nights that never grew heavy with humid air, the only good thing about her time in Turner Hill.

Feeling better now, she donned a lightweight blouse and her split riding skirt. Pulling her hair up at the nape of her neck, she secured it with a ribbon and then set a straw-brimmed hat onto her head.

Downstairs, she filled a jar with lemonade, and when she walked outside she found Clint waiting in front of the house holding the reins of two horses, Sunshine and Midnight.

She handed him the lemonade and watched as he placed it into a saddlebag and tightened the strap. He turned to her. "Ready?"

She nodded and mounted Sunshine with his help. Having him touch her was becoming far too familiar.

Yet each brush of his hands brought a thrill to her system. She couldn't escape it, though there were a thousand reasons she should.

Once she was seated with reins in hand, she watched him mount the gelding in one fluid movement, his leg lifting up and over until he sat upright, as if one with the animal. The slightest nudge from him sent Midnight into a walk. Sunshine followed and they headed away from the house, toward the creek.

She reminded herself this wasn't a Sunday-afternoon ride with a beau. They wouldn't picnic by the water and play silly games, laughing the afternoon away.

Yet she grew excited with anticipation and pretended, just for a time, that it were truly the case.

Chapter Nine

Midnight led and Sunshine followed. The new mama mare was ready for light exercise. Clint made sure to keep an easy pace for Tess's mount, and they followed a path leading them out of the yard, back behind the house, where tall green grass had faded and withered some from the summer sun. They rode through a wild-apple orchard and farther to where the path was worn and wide and easy to track even with untrained eyes.

He heard the rush of the creek first and breathed in the scent of fresh water next. The path opened up to a broad expanse of old, tired oaks. Twisted branches reached out and over the creek to touch and mingle with the neighboring trees on the opposite bank.

"My father," he began, gazing out at the view before him, "wanted to have this creek on his property. He'd settled this parcel of land *because* of it. I haven't seen it since I've been back."

He didn't know why he shared that with Tess. Usually he kept the history of the Double H to himself.

"Your father often spoke of it, Clint," Tess said, reining Sunshine close. "When I met him he wasn't strong enough to come here. After he died I came by myself once to see this place. It's beautiful."

"He married my mother here."

Tess held her gaze steady on him, covering her surprise, but he'd seen the quick flicker in her eyes and the slight shift of her body atop the mare.

"Guess he forgot to tell you that. And all the promises he'd made my mother that day."

Tess spoke quietly, "I knew this was a special place to him. He spoke fondly of this creek, Clint. Can't you see that he did care about you and your mother?"

Clint held his tongue and rode deeper into the shaded area, where the ground sloped to the creek's bank. He dismounted and turned to her. She was right behind and he helped her down, releasing her quickly, his emotions reeling.

He'd wanted Tess to see this place, where vows of love and honor had taken place. He'd wanted her with him the first time he came back here and he wasn't certain why that was exactly.

"Why am I here?" she asked, directing those clear blue eyes at him asking him the same question he'd asked himself.

He walked to the creek's bank and stared as the sun, laced through interlocking branches, cast a shimmer of light onto the low rushing waters. He shook his head. "I don't trust you."

He heard the sound of her footsteps and figured she'd retreated, back to Sunshine, ready to leave the creek.

But when he turned around, she stood before him, her face a picture of beautiful confusion. She spoke softly. "I don't know that I trust you, either."

"Fair enough," he said, taking in the fragrant scent of roses. Flushed from heat, her cheeks were bright with color, and the few tendrils escaping the protection of her straw hat were moist at her nape. Clint had the urge to nibble on that area at the back of her neck and lick the small beads with his tongue.

His desire for her had nothing to do with trusting her. He understood they had doubts and misgivings regarding each other. "But if I were to tell you I'm not behind the sabotage at the ranch, could you believe me?"

Tess put her lips together and darted a glance toward the cool waters, contemplating. She lifted her gaze back to him. "I'm not sure."

He'd expected that. "Hell, you're honest…*about that.*"

Tess glanced away again and something again flickered in her eyes. Then she looked at him squarely. "Can you believe that I haven't done anything to sabotage the ranch either?"

Clint cocked her a quick smile. "I'm trying."

He walked over to Midnight and reached into his

saddlebag. Lifting out the jar of lemonade, he unscrewed the top. Then he approached her again, offering up the lemonade and a bargain. "I think we should work together. Try to figure this out. That fire was a close call. It seems the attacks are getting more dangerous. And I've got a notion that whoever is doing this has firsthand knowledge of the ranch."

She took the offered jar from his hands. "You believe it's someone who works for the Double H?"

Clint nodded. "It makes sense. And it may be more than one person. They know how to hurt us and when to do it."

"Do you have any idea who it is?"

Again he sent a smile her way. "You mean, now that I know it's not you?"

"It's not me," she said without hesitation. She took a long sip of lemonade and handed the bottle back to him.

He looked at it and placed his mouth where hers had touched. The scent of her lingered on the bottle, and he drank up heartily, never remembering enjoying lemonade quite so much. "And it's not me."

Her brows bowed prettily. "I haven't conceded that point yet."

Setting the bottle back into the saddlebag, he scrubbed his jaw and took note of her stubborn nature. "Just listen up. It has to be someone who works on the Double H. An outsider would be too easily noticed. So we're gonna have to watch everyone closely. I mean *everyone,* Tess."

She closed her eyes briefly.

He took hold of her upper arms. "Can you do that?"

She stared at him and he saw a quick battle wage on her expression. Then she nodded. "I'll do whatever it takes to keep the ranch out of trouble."

Though he'd gotten the answer he wanted, he frowned at her blind dedication to the ranch. It only made his cause more difficult. "Don't let on what we're doing. We want whoever's doing this to make a mistake. It's the only way we'll catch them."

Tess cast him a guarded look. "I hope you're right. Not about the culprit being a trusted employee—I'd hate to see that. But this should stop before someone gets hurt."

"You need to trust me, Tess."

She'd been hurt, and the pain from the past went deep. That much Clint knew just from good instincts. But he needed her trust now if they were ever going to move on. While the problems at the ranch should have discouraged and weakened her, making his plan to buy her out more appealing, she'd dug her heels in and stood firm, stubbornly refusing to let it sway her.

"I'll work with you, Clint. Because for once it seems we have the same purpose. But don't ask any more of me right now. Until you understand I'll never betray the promise I made your father, I *can't* be on your side entirely."

Clint freed her arms but kept a vigil on her face. "Agreed."

She let go a shaky smile.

"We have a truce then?" He put out his hand.

A moment ticked by.

She set her hand in his, ready for the deal-making pump. But instead of a shake, he laced their fingers and squeezed gently. She gazed into his eyes, watching him. When she didn't resist the contact, he lowered his mouth to hers, waiting for her retreat. Waiting to see if she'd pull away from him.

He'd been eager to hold her again, to feel the brush of her body against his. He'd kissed her once and determined it was too good not to do again.

"A truce," she whispered.

He wound their entwined hands behind her back and tugged her closer. When he set his lips to hers he was greeted by soft, willing acceptance.

He covered her mouth, claiming her in a kiss that started out easy. She flowed into him, and her little moan of pleasure had him wanting to lay her down on the grassy slope.

He deepened the kiss, enjoying the taste of her, lemony-tart and soft and delicious. His senses reeled from her female fragrance that seemed to blend with the earth, the creek and the oaks. His groin reacted and he restrained his desire, taking his time, slowly bending her to his will.

She kissed him back until she was breathless, her hips moving in slow, passionate circles, pressing him, driving him toward the edge of insanity.

They mated their tongues and Clint tasted her

more thoroughly, exploring the sweetness of her mouth. He moved his hands over her backside, stroking her, feeling the perfection of her round cheeks and cupping her in each palm.

"Clint," she murmured.

It was neither a plea nor a warning but more a word spoken in awe. He felt the same as sensations rippled through him. He didn't rush the feeling but savored each new exploration of her body.

He looked at her face, her eyes dewy, her cheeks flaming and her lips ripe and full. Clint had never wanted a woman more than he wanted Tess.

She was the enemy.

She was a woman who stood in the way of his goals.

But she was soft and giving and he knew he had to thread carefully. The restraint was killing him.

He took the hat off her head and tossed it aside. Then he untied the ribbon at the nape of her neck and spread her hair over her shoulders, watching silky strawberry strands cascade through his fingers.

He swallowed when he saw her breaths come quickly, her breathing as stirred up as his.

He flattened his palm to her throat, felt her rapid pulse there. Then he moved farther down, his fingers nimbly undoing the top button on her blouse. When she didn't protest, Clint kissed her again and continued to unfasten each button. Placing his hands inside, he separated the material enough to reach up and pull the chemise straps down, exposing two plump, beautiful mounds of flesh.

He sucked in oxygen. Then looked into her eyes. "Do you know how beautiful you are?"

She shook her head. Confusion and lust were a heady combination on the face of a gorgeous woman.

"I'm about to show you."

She closed her eyes and Clint took that as her full compliance. He touched her breasts with open palms, splaying his fingers wide.

Pure desire raced through his body, igniting him to hot flames.

She snapped her eyes open with a look of hesitation. "Clint."

"Don't be afraid of me. You know this will only bring you pleasure."

He planted tiny kisses on her lips and then thumbed over one nipple, making it peak to a rosy bud.

"I'm not afraid," she breathed out.

"Good thing." He kissed her again, then nibbled on her chin, her throat and lower, to the valley between her breasts.

When he took her into his mouth and suckled, she gasped aloud, and it wasn't fear he heard but surprise and wonder.

He smiled to himself. He, too, was surprised at the intensity of his desire, but his only wonder was at how he'd managed to keep away from her, from doing this, for so long. He'd rather set her down on a soft feather bed, but the shaded green grass wasn't such a terrible alternative, not when he had a willing woman in his arms.

He unbuttoned his shirt, longing to feel her delicate fingers slide across his chest, and once the shirt was off, he set her hands on him. "Touch me, Tess."

She stared at him for a moment, and he encouraged her with a slight nod and, covering her hands, showed her what he wanted.

She moved her hands over him tentatively, unsure of her actions, it seemed, but her slight hesitations only added to his rising desire, making him want more.

"It's gonna be good between us, honey."

He tried to slip her blouse from her shoulders, but she gripped it tight and shook her head as if she'd just come to some stark, dreadful realization. "No, I can't do this."

Clint struggled with impatience. "We're partway there, Tess. Don't deny what you want."

"Oh, God," she said, biting her lip and pulling up her chemise straps, covering her luscious body.

"You want this as much as I do."

Her silence was enough to convince him.

"I'm not a bully, Tess. If you haven't been with a man in a while, I'll be tender." He wouldn't bring his father's name into this conversation, though he suspected she might have had other lovers before Hoyt—and maybe after him, as well.

Tess blinked. "I'm sorry."

"You're *sorry?*" Clint nearly choked at her apology.

"Yes," she said quietly, her eyes welling with tears.

Clint couldn't take a woman's tears. They brought him to his knees. Right now he was damn frustrated and confused, and Tess crying would only irritate him more. "Hell, don't cry!"

She stopped her tears as if she'd drawn on some past memory on how to do it. Quickly and obediently. Clint knew she'd had a rough young life, but it was even more evident now, seeing her retreat both physically and emotionally.

She'd tempted him beyond reason and sanity. She'd let him touch her in ways that she knew would lead to only one thing. If it had been an act, then she would earn an award for a convincing performance, because she'd responded to him like a woman ready to be taken.

Had she enticed him deliberately, giving him notions of bedding her to tempt and torture him? Was she that devious and cunning? He gritted his teeth. "You little tease. Is this what you do? Tempt a man into heaven to get what you want? Is that how you got my father to marry you?"

"I'm not a tease," she said defiantly, her eyes snapping wide, blazing hot. "And I'm through explaining my relationship with Hoyt to you."

She'd refastened her blouse in the time she'd taken to say those words. Her hair mussed, her lips swollen, she kept her head down as she walked away, refusing to look at him as she mounted Sunshine.

He grabbed the mare's reins to gain Tess's attention. She looked at him from atop the horse.

"Don't play dangerous games when you don't know the rules. You'll lose every time," he warned.

"I know the rules." She spoke confidently, yet her expression was a mixture of sadness and regret. There was an unguarded look in her eyes that went straight to his gut like a cowpoke's punch in a saloon brawl.

Sunshine shifted her stance, rearing back a step. Clint spoke a soft command and the mare stilled immediately.

Tess reached down for the reins. "I've got to go back."

He relinquished the reins, and she snared them quickly and turned Sunshine around. She rode the mare toward the house as Clint watched in amazement.

"Damn it, Tess," he muttered because, strangely, he believed her.

She hadn't been teasing him today, though temptation sat between them, unsatisfied. Her responses were passionate and honest, Clint wasn't mistaken. Both felt the attraction like the pull of a powerful river.

Something had stopped her. She was running scared. He'd be damned if he could figure out what had brought on her tears and her retreat.

Denying them both a good deal of pleasure.

Tess rode Sunshine at a quickened pace, tears she couldn't shed in front of Clint now raining down her cheeks. Once she was far enough away from the creek, she slowed the mare, remembering she was a new mama and could tire easily.

She'd made a truce with Clint today, for the ranch's sake, and she felt it'd been the only decision she could make. Though her lips still tasted of him, her body still hummed from his touch, she knew she'd made a bad decision allowing him those liberties.

Clint wasn't to be trusted. Not with her heart.

As much as she wanted to keep him at arm's length to protect all that she'd struggled for these past months, he'd managed to slip in beyond her defenses.

She felt something for him.

She cared.

He'd been gentle with her, his touch striking a chord within her, igniting her passion and creating thrilling havoc in her body. His kisses were heated, his lips commanding and guiding and encouraging, but Clint never overwhelmed her by taking away her control. He knew that she needed to have that freedom. He understood. He'd always given her a choice.

Touching him had been glorious. He was broad of chest and well muscled, defining the infinite days of hard work in a rancher's life. Under her fingertips she'd felt his strength and itched to feel more of him—to touch him intimately.

When she looked at him, the dark gleam of desire in his eyes almost melted away every chunk of her resolve.

He was a beautiful man.

With a heart of stone, she reminded herself.

Clint wasn't to be trusted. That's what perplexed her most. He was out to destroy something precious, and if she got in his way, no doubt she'd be discarded as quickly as a heap of rotting rubbish.

Tess had only known men who'd used and abused people. In some ways, Clint wasn't too different from Frank and Rusty Metcalf. He took what he wanted, no matter the cost to others, without conscience or regret.

Except for Hoyt, she'd never had a decent, caring relationship with a man. Certainly only a foolish woman would entertain thoughts of loving strong, determined, hard-hearted Clint Hayworth.

So, as tender as Clint might have been, as much as she'd wanted him, she'd made the correct decision in stopping Clint's advances. She'd learned to trust her instincts and place value on herself. But leaving Clint behind at the creek hadn't been easy.

He thought her a tease and a wanton woman.

He was wrong on both accounts.

She'd wanted to have something real and something solid with a man who would love her. But long ago she had given up that dream.

The Double H was her something solid now. She'd do her utmost to keep it safe and to keep the Hayworth name held in high regard.

Drying her tears and sitting taller in the saddle, she came to a startling revelation: this time she wasn't protecting the ranch for Hoyt but for herself.

She was a Hayworth now, through and through.

A few days later Tess stood before nearly thirty women seated in the dining room at the Hayworth Hotel. She'd managed to put aside thoughts of her time with Clint at the creek in order to concentrate on this meeting. The distraction had been well timed. She'd spent far too much time thinking of him lately, remembering how his touch had thrilled and excited her.

She'd avoided him on the ranch whenever she could, but she knew that wouldn't last. They had shared responsibilities. So far, he hadn't pressed her about the truce she'd made with him. Sooner or later they'd have to plan their strategy and work together to protect the Hayworth holdings.

Now she looked at the curious faces of the women in attendance. Their ages ranged from younger, more innocent girls to older women who'd had many life experiences.

Tess fit somewhere in between. Robbed of the innocence of youth, she'd had to grow up quicker than most young girls. She hoped HELP would do that very thing—help women who were going through similar experiences.

She looked out at the women and smiled with warmth and a measure of trepidation. This idea had become very important to her, and she wanted so desperately to find common ground with all who attended. "Welcome, ladies. This is the first meeting of Hayworth's Exceptional Ladies Partnership. I hope to have many more to come. Please have your tea and sample some of the hotel's desserts while I explain to you why we're all here."

"First I'll tell you a little about myself. I had one brother and was raised by my father. I lost my mother at a very young age. When I needed to feel close to her I would take up the only thing I had to remind me of her—a beautiful silk embroidered handkerchief. In troubled times, I'd clutch it in my hand and say a prayer, and in those moments I'd feel better. The handkerchief was lost to me when I was fourteen, but the memory of it always stayed with me. It would lend me peace and consolation."

Tess recalled the bitter moment when her father had gotten angry with her for dropping a basket of eggs on the ground. He'd ranted at her stupidity and slapped her face, then pulled the handkerchief from where she'd concealed it every day, tucked under the wrist of her sleeve. He'd ripped it deliberately and tossed it into the morning fire.

Tess had sobbed inconsolably watching it burn up, the three perfectly embroidered red roses she'd finger with love each night before bed going up in flames.

Tess allowed that memory to flash for only a second. She picked up the stack of wrapped gifts and moved around the room, handing each woman a prettily tied package.

"These are replicas, from memory, and my way of thanking you all for coming here today. I hope the gift gives you some joy…and some peace."

When she reached Marla and Pearl, the two females sitting next to one another, she reassured them with a smile. The women both cast her hesitant smiles in return.

Tess finished giving out the gifts and noted that Laura hadn't yet arrived. She'd been responsible for commissioning three seamstresses to embroider the blooming crimson roses on each of the silk handkerchiefs. Laura had promised to be here today and Tess worried at her absence.

She reached the front of the dining room again and noted the women's expressions were slightly more at ease.

She began, "I know this meeting takes many of you away from your chores and—"

"I don't mind missing my chores," one of the older women said.

Chuckles resounded in the room as many others agreed.

Tess grinned. "This is not a suffrage meeting, ladies, or a women's social, but a sisterhood."

Many of the women looked confused, while others nodded their understanding. "I'd like us to simply share ideas and thoughts on being a woman in Hayworth. To help us realize that, as women, we have certain obligations to our families, but we also have certain rights. To start with, I'd like to tell you a little about my childhood and then I'd like to ask you a question."

Tess spoke for twenty minutes, explaining how she was raised by a cruel father and how she'd witnessed her brother's beatings. She spoke of how her father belittled her and made her feel worthless as a child. She spoke from her heart, but she didn't have the courage to speak the entire truth. She couldn't quite bring herself to confess she'd been a sister to a murdering outlaw. She couldn't admit that she'd shot and killed her own brother.

She continued to live the lie of Tess Morgan Hayworth. She rationalized that if she could help women in similar circumstances stand up for themselves, then hiding her true identity would be justified.

When she finished speaking, she was drained emotionally. For most of her life she'd kept those awful memories buried. She'd rarely spoken of them, not in detail, not even to Hoyt. Today she'd uncovered some truths that had held her hostage. Instead of feeling ashamed, as she had in the past, she held her head high, realizing that she wasn't at fault. She'd been born to a kindhearted mother who'd died far too young and a father who hadn't an ounce of humanity in him.

She felt cleansed somewhat and relieved that she'd spoken part of her truth here today. Amazingly, when she'd set up this meeting she'd thought to help others, but it appeared obvious that she was gaining a good deal of help herself. The revelation struck a chord in her and brought her joy.

"Now, ladies, ask yourselves, have you ever been in a situation like mine? Have you ever wished you were treated with more respect? Wished you'd been treated more kindly?"

Tess glanced around the room to stony looks. She reached out to meet each woman's eyes, searching for a response, a gesture, but the dining room was as silent as a funeral procession.

It occurred to Tess that if she couldn't sway a

response, the assembly would soon be over. The women weren't talking.

Then Pearl spoke up, her eyes darting about the room before meeting with Tess's gaze. "I have, Mrs. Hayworth. I've wished many a time to have more respect from my man."

Tess knew what it cost Pearl to be the first to speak up. She wanted to run over to her and hug her, but instead she smiled at her with heartfelt gratitude, and Pearl accepted that. "Thank you, Pearl. Anyone else?"

As soon as Pearl had cleared the path, other women joined in. Though they didn't go into any detail, they'd started talking more freely.

This is what Tess wanted to accomplish. She wanted women to feel free enough to speak out, to have someone to listen to their misgivings and troubles without fear. And she gave a reminder to all present. "Please, ladies, whatever you hear in this room should be kept private. This meeting is about respect and sisterhood. This is a *partnership*. We want this to be a place where all of you can share your thoughts freely. Nothing you hear in this room should be repeated."

Though Laura had warned her that some women were downright busybodies, Tess had faith that the women would recognize the need to keep their silence. And then she made the one offer she hoped she would never have to entertain. "Ladies, please, if any one of you ever needs help, seek out a friend. There's nothing worse that having those dreadful feelings of despair and having to hold them inside. If you're hurt or hurting, my home is open to all of you. I will listen to you, and together we'll work through your troubles. Please, anytime. Come see me."

Tess ended the meeting by asking the women if they'd feel it worthwhile to continue to get together, and all of the women agreed. She set a date for the next meeting, encouraging them to come.

As the ladies began to exit the hotel, a dozen women crowded her and thanked her personally. One of them was the girl Marla had spoken about. She had a bruise on her arm that Tess couldn't miss. She hugged each of them before they left and sent up a prayer for the women she knew, by the fearful looks in their eyes, were the ones who needed help.

Tess left the hotel by midafternoon and was walking toward the livery when she spotted Tom across the street, rocking little Abby in his arms as he made his way to the *Herald* office. "Tom," she called out, waving her arm.

Tom stopped to turn, and when he saw her he walked across the street.

She couldn't contain her excitement at seeing Abby again. "Oh, let me hold her, Tom."

Tom relinquished his hold on the baby, easily handing her over to Tess. "Where's Laura?" she asked, looking into the baby's blue eyes and rocking her gently. "She didn't make our meeting today."

Tom frowned. "She's been…tired. I took the baby from her this afternoon so she could rest."

"Tired? It's been a while now since the birth. Shouldn't she be feeling stronger by now?"

"Dr. Willis says she's fine. Nothing wrong that he can tell. I thought it'd do her good for me to take the baby for a few hours."

"Oh, let me, Tom! I'll take her for a while and you can get back to work."

Tom looked so relieved that Tess wondered if there wasn't something else wrong, but she didn't pry. "Would you?" he asked. "I have an article to write and I've never missed a deadline."

"Of course! Little Abby and I will find something to do."

"She really likes being outdoors. Laura hasn't taken her out much."

"Well, then, I know just the place. I'll take her over to the church grounds. We'll sit in the shady meadow, and after a while I'll take her back to your house. I'd planned on seeing Laura today anyway."

"Gosh, Tess, thanks. You'd really be helping me out."

"Go then, Tom. Don't worry about Abby."

Tom bent to kiss his daughter on the forehead. "You be a good girl for your Aunt Tess, now. Bye-bye, sweet cheeks."

Tess laughed at the adorable nickname as she watched Tom head back to the newspaper office. Then she took off with the baby, glad to be of help to Tom and even happier to get a chance to spend time with Abby.

* * *

Clint watched and waited during the entire week, hoping to uncover something about the calamities occurring on the Double H. He'd spent time with the ranch hands, spoken with each of the rotating guards at night, worked with the smithy, helped put a roof on the new supply shed and spent time with Sunset. At least he'd made a bit of progress gaining the stallion's trust.

Clint leaned up against a tree, watching Sunset, learning about him, discovering little by little his movements, his frustration and his habits. The stallion still had rage in him. He'd prance and pace and snort his fury. Clint couldn't blame him. The animal wanted his freedom. He wanted off the Double H ranch and to get back to his herd. So many times Clint watched him from afar as Sunset looked at the high corral fence as if wondering if he could make the jump. Could he clear the last rung of the fence? All that separated him from what he wanted most stood over five feet high and rounded the perimeter of the corral.

Clint understood his desire to be free. He'd let him go if he thought the stallion would survive another winter. But his herd ran wild on the mesas of Palo Duro Canyon, where grazing land was sparse and dry, and fresh water in short supply. Herds in that area struggled with disease and starvation. Clint recalled seeing those dying animals as a young boy when he'd venture that far up the mesa with his friends, and the heartbreaking images had stayed with him.

He pushed his hat up his forehead and walked over to the corral, garnering the stallion's wary attention. "It's all right, boy," he called out, making eye contact. "Nothing to be nervous about."

He opened the gate and let himself in, keeping a vigil on the horse's movements. He could only push him so far. Clint hadn't come up against an animal so hard to tame. And he'd tamed some wild ones back in Houston. He'd made a living working with spirited stallions and training them, then selling them to owners who would value their intelligence and worth.

He'd gotten completely out of the cattle business, and that's where he wanted to stay. Working the Double H had been ingrained in him from early on, and at one time he'd thought it was his birthright to run the Hayworth empire. Clint knew better now. He knew what brought him a sense of accomplishment and satisfaction.

Last week Sunset charged him when he'd jumped into the corral, and now the stallion tolerated his being inside so long as he stayed by the opposing fence.

Clint stood inside for a few minutes more than he had the day before. Tomorrow he'd stay a bit longer, and then longer again, until Sunset became familiar with his being inside. Each day he'd step a little closer toward him. Each day he'd stay calm and patient, waiting the stallion out.

He timed his stay and then retreated, keeping eye contact with the horse as he exited the corral and latched the gate.

"It's all right, boy," he repeated. "You see? Nothing to get nervous about."

He spoke in the same tone every day, allowing the stallion to recognize the sound of his voice. Gaining his trust.

He figured making a truce with a wild stallion would be easier than making one with Tess.

Though they lived in the same house, Clint had seen very little of Tess since their time by the creek. Clint caught glimpses of her during the day, but she seemed deep in thought and busier than usual. They'd spoken only a few words, all related to ranch business. Neither one had discovered anything more about the calamities at the ranch lately.

But one day midweek Clint had gone into town early in the afternoon with a few of the ranch hands to pick up supplies. The boys ventured on to the saloon for a drink, but Clint was ill at ease about leaving the ranch for too long. He left town straight-away by himself, and on his way out he'd caught sight of Tess sitting on a soft patch of grass at the church, cradling a baby in her arms.

He'd figured it was Laura's child. But by all accounts, the baby could have been Tess's, from the way she held that child to her chest, peering down with love and swaying her body to rock the child to sleep.

The scene she made with that baby loosened something in his heart. Initially it didn't look right seeing that child in her arms, but as he'd continued to watch her from the cover of a tall willow, he'd found it looked more than right on Tess.

It looked perfect.

No, I'm not the motherly kind.

He recalled her admission to him. Had that been a lie?

And what did it matter to him if she did have motherly tendencies?

Yet, he'd left town that day with a feeling in his gut that wouldn't quit niggling at him.

At night, Clint would walk past her bedroom door, where he pictured her sleeping alone in that big bed. He'd stop and listen, sorely tempted to enter the room and take her into his arms.

There was a connection between them that was created by a contest of wills over the Double H. Yet his desire for her went beyond a need to bed his father's widow. Though that would be sweet revenge, it didn't matter to him who she was or when or where they'd met, Clint would want her.

He'd had a taste of her passion.

And now he wanted it all.

Chapter Ten

Later that week Clint couldn't contain his bad mood. He slammed the front door and strode into the house, catching a glimpse of Tess seated in the parlor, knitting.

Seeing her that way, with head down, concentrating over a pink baby blanket, only irritated him more. He'd been thinking about her all day, and the lusty images he'd pictured in his mind didn't come close to the tranquil scene before him.

He leaned on the door frame, watching her cross one needle over the other, making stitches. In the past, his mother had sat on that very chair, knitting for her family. His gut churned seeing the redheaded widow do the same. The maternal scene struck him. Tess had no business looking so damn domestic. "Practicing for when you snare your next rich husband?"

She didn't react to his comment. She kept on creating stitches. "I'm making a blanket for baby Abby."

Set on her task, there was serenity in her voice, and her expression was one of peace and joy.

The same damn expression that had knocked him to his knees when he saw her in the church meadow, holding the baby in her arms.

For a moment Clint's foul mood ebbed. He watched her.

"Is there something you want?" she asked, still concentrating on the blanket.

"I had to fire Jeb Sweeny today."

She stopped knitting and looked up.

"We had us...a little problem."

Tess set her knitting aside and stood. "What kind of problem?" She approached him, her gaze falling to his mouth. "And why is your lip bleeding?"

Clint touched his sore lip and came away with a drop of blood. Before he could reach for his bandanna, Tess produced a handkerchief from her skirt pocket. She dabbed at his lip with soft-eyed concern. "Are you going to tell me why I see blood on your shirt? Or shall I ask Sonny?"

Clint grabbed the kerchief from her hand. "Nah... don't ask Sonny."

She looked at him with curious eyes. "As far as I know, Jeb's been a good worker. He's been on the payroll for two years. What happened, Clint?"

"I slammed my fist in his face."

Tess gasped, but she recovered quickly. "He must have gotten in a shot, too, or you wouldn't be bleeding."

Clint frowned. A flowery fragrance filled the room

and brought back memories of being with Tess at the creek, breathing in her sweet scent and touching her in ways he wanted to repeat again.

"Lucky shot. After that it was all over."

"You still haven't told me why."

He didn't want to tell her, but he figured if he didn't, then she'd find out by Sonny or one of the other men. He couldn't trust their accounting of the incident.

Clint wondered at the wisdom of what he'd done, but there was no taking it back. He'd do it all over again if he had to. "Let's just say Jeb had notions that I didn't agree with."

Tess looked puzzled. Her brows gathered as she waited for his explanation. When Clint hesitated, she breathed out, "For heaven's sake, Clint. Just tell me."

Sonny entered the room. "He was protecting your honor, Tess."

She hadn't heard the ranch foreman come into the house. He nodded and looked at Clint. "Jeb got a little outta line and Clint—"

"He got *a lot* outta line," Clint said, still angry at Jeb's assumptions.

Tess looked from Clint to Sonny and back. "Protecting my *honor?*"

Sonny rubbed his cheek, frowning. "This ain't easy to say out loud. But, uh, Jeb—"

"Damn it, Sonny. I'll tell it." Clint sent him a long, hard stare and Sonny backed off.

"Okay, then. Tell it, boy. I'll just go get myself one of Greta's Berliners."

Tess folded her arms around her middle and waited. "Clint?"

With Sonny out of the room, Clint figured he'd just lay it on the line. "I overheard him telling the men that if the boss wasn't bedding you by now, then he wanted a chance at the widow. He mentioned something about courting you, but by then my fist was in his face, so I didn't hear the rest."

Tess staggered back. Color drained from her face. She got that look again, the one that he'd only seen in her most unguarded moments, as if recalling bad memories. "Oh…I see."

"He's already gone. I watched him pack his gear and ride off the property."

In that moment Tess seemed to snap out of whatever she'd been thinking. Her color came back and she straightened her spine. "I don't approve of violence, Clint."

"He got what was coming." Clint damn well wasn't about to apologize or make excuses for what he'd done. As it was, he'd sugarcoated what Jeb had said to spare Tess from hearing the vile words spoken.

"Did you break his nose?"

"Maybe. Blood spurted out everywhere."

Tess took a better inspection of his bloodstained shirt. "Oh, God." Then she looked at him in earnest. "You've spoken worse about me without blinking. I don't understand why you defended me."

Clint had asked himself that a dozen times before he'd come inside the house to tell her about firing Jeb.

Something just snapped inside him when he heard the ranch hand talking about Tess that way. Clint had reacted out of anger and jealousy and that's what irritated him the most. Knowing he'd have to admit the truth to her added to his bad mood.

He'd lost a good worker today. Jeb would be hard to replace, but Clint had wanted him off Double H land as quickly as possible.

"Wasn't so much defending you as teaching the boys about respecting their boss and the Double H."

Tess put her lips together nearly in a smile. "So you fired him for the *ranch's* sake?"

Was she mocking him? He set his face in a scowl. "Damn waste of a clean shirt."

Tess eyed his bloody shirt again, then looked up to meet his gaze directly. "When are you going to see the truth, Clint? You care about this ranch. And maybe you care about me…just a little."

"Don't put words in my mouth. Firing Jeb had nothing to do with you."

She cast him a knowing look. "It was about *respect?*"

He set his stance firm. "I said it was."

"Still doesn't make sense. Why would you care about the crew respecting me or the *ranch* when it's clear that you don't?"

Clint didn't have an answer. He'd reacted from instinct. He didn't like the notion of Jeb Sweeny anywhere near Tess. The last thing he'd allow to happen was for Tess to take a lover.

Unless it was him.

Tess sat and picked up her knitting, pretty much dismissing him.

He spun around and strode out of the room, Tess's final comment before he walked out the door ringing in his ears.

"There's hope for you yet, Clint Hayworth."

It was like the quiet before the storm. Tess didn't trust *calm.* She had too many memories of her childhood, when all seemed almost normal in the Metcalf home, then out of nowhere her father would erupt into a rage. Her brother Rusty would take the brunt of his tirade, while a younger Theresa would retreat to the corner, trying to hide, to crawl into herself as she cried her eyes out.

Those feelings never ebbed, and lately she'd been sensing something else coming on. She hadn't expected the problem with Jeb Sweeny yesterday or Clint's reaction to him. That had surprised her. But other than Clint's firing of Jeb, there hadn't been any incidents on the ranch this week that should give her cause for alarm.

But she felt it.

A certain gnawing unease.

She took a bite of her supper, Greta's specialty of red cabbage and roasted beef, and listened to her speak about her brother who'd lived in Germany and had settled in the east. Tess appreciated Greta's slight warming to her. At times it seemed Greta even liked

Tess, but she wasn't an easy woman to impress, and Tess had decided to let things be. They'd come to terms in their own way. Greta wasn't a woman who befriended easily, but when she did you had a friend for life. Tess wasn't leaving the ranch, so she'd bide her time and let their relationship develop gradually, over time.

Tess finished her supper and knew better than to help Greta clean up the kitchen. The cook wouldn't hear of it, and Tess had finally learned to respect her wishes.

Small steps.

She strode down the hallway and past the staircase, ready to pick up her knitting in the parlor, when a hard, pounding knock on the front door startled her. She walked over to the door and opened it. Randy stood on the threshold, his face red, his breathing labored. "Got here as fast as I could."

The quiet hadn't lasted. Something was terribly wrong. "What is it?"

"Got this note from Mr. Larson in town. He said to give it to you pronto, Mrs. Hayworth. It's important." He handed her the note.

"Thank you, Randy. Why don't you go into the kitchen? Greta will give you a cold lemonade."

She was on her way to the parlor to read the note before she'd spoken those last words. Unfolding the paper with hands she willed not to tremble, she read it silently. *Tess, come quick. Meet me in the secret meeting place. I need to see you alone. Tom.*

Tess dropped the note on the floor, her mind racing. Her sense of dread had just been answered and, oddly, she wasn't surprised. But she hadn't expected the problem to stem from Tom. He would never have summoned her to town this late in the day if he weren't desperate.

"Randy!" she called out. He was there in an instant, waiting for her instructions. "Saddle up Maple. I need to go into town."

"Yes, ma'am. Right away."

Tess didn't have time to think any further. She ran upstairs, put on her riding clothes—a split skirt and a cotton blouse—and covered her shoulders with a light wrap.

Without hesitation, she left the house before dusk settled onto the Double H ranch.

Clint watched from a distance, making sure Tess couldn't see him sitting on his horse, hidden behind tall brush on a ridge. A short time ago he'd come into the house looking for her and found a note on the floor from Tom instead.

Meet me in the secret meeting place. I need to see you alone.

Clint had followed her. Hadn't been hard. Not as hard as realizing he'd been duped. He'd pegged her deceit right from the beginning. But somewhere along the line he'd begun to think he'd been wrong about her. Somewhere along the line he'd begun to think she wasn't the hard-hearted, money-grubbing woman he'd convinced himself she was when he'd first arrived at the Double H.

Now he saw the foolishness in that.

Clint ground his teeth watching Tess pace by the stream. And his hands fisted when Tom Larson walked up and seemed relieved to see her.

Tom Larson? He'd married Tess's best friend, Laura. The woman had just had his child. Clint couldn't reconcile this in his mind. He'd thought the worst of Tess when she married an elderly, sick man in order to get her hands on his money, but even he hadn't thought she'd betray her friend.

Tom took Tess in his arms and they embraced.

Clint had seen enough.

He rode toward town, tamping down rage that would have him confronting her. She'd been caught, and there wasn't a doubt in his mind now that Tess was behind the accidents at the ranch. He'd almost believed in her innocence. He'd almost given her that much trust, but now it was all clear.

She had an accomplice. That made all things possible.

She wanted Clint off the ranch. She liked her status as the rich, powerful widow of Hoyt Hayworth. Wouldn't do to have the townsfolk find out she'd taken a lover so soon after Hoyt's death. He wondered how many times she'd met with Tom secretly. And how they'd thought to deceive him by causing one ruckus after another on the ranch.

Hell, they probably hadn't planned on his

showing up at all after his father died. And when he did, they'd concocted this scheme knowing that Clint didn't have any fondness for the ranch. Did they believe he'd turn tail and run at the first hint of trouble?

Clint ground his teeth thinking of all those nights he'd stopped by Tess's bedroom door, picturing her unclothed and sprawled out on the bed. He'd been plagued with images of touching her again, kissing her senseless and driving himself into her body until both were exhausted and completely sated.

Clint rode Midnight hard. He reached the Hayworth Saloon with a bitter taste in his mouth. He dismounted, tethering his horse, aiming to wipe that taste out with a bottle of Jack Daniel's ninety-proof bourbon.

As he strode toward the bar, Micah Willits slapped him on the back. "Good to see you in town, Clint."

Clint was in no mood for pleasantries. He nodded to the rancher and continued on. Another man took his hand in a shake. "Mr. Hayworth, let me say how sorry I am for your father's passing. Mr. Hayworth paid my bills when my little Joanie took sick."

Clint accepted his thanks with another nod of his head, figuring Hoyt must have had a self-serving reason to help the man, but he kept that notion to himself.

Finally, when he reached the polished dark oak counter, the barkeep greeted him, wiping a shot glass clean. "Howdy, Mr. Hayworth. What can I do for you?"

Clint leaned on the counter. "A bottle of your best bourbon."

"Sure thing. Want to sit yourself down at a table? I'll bring it—"

"Nope. Just a bottle and a glass."

Clint didn't know the barkeep. He hadn't much cause to come to town. But the man worked for him, and Clint had seen his name on the payroll.

Hoyt Hayworth built this saloon right after he sold his first hundred head of beeves. Of course, Clint remembered the saloon looking different, smaller, less stylish. Over the years everything Hayworth owned eventually was improved upon until it set the standard for all others.

That was how his father had done business. Being the biggest, being the best, meant the most to him.

Clint poured his first shot and swallowed it in one gulp. Amber fire burned his throat. He relished the sensation.

"Tell me," he said to the barkeep, rolling the small glass around in hands. "Do you know Tom Larson?"

"Yes, sir."

Clint looked up. "What'd you think of him?"

The barkeep's light brows rose and he didn't hesitate. "He's a good man. Fair. Honest."

Clint poured a second time and took another swallow of bourbon. "That's how I remembered him, too." Clint had known Tom while growing up. Tom had been book-smart. He'd always had his nose in a reader. And he'd never gotten himself in any trouble.

Tess was enough temptation for any man. Maybe

she'd worked her wiles on him. Or maybe the earnest bookworm Clint remembered as a boy had changed. People do. They change due to the circumstances in their lives.

Didn't matter, though. The man Clint once knew wasn't the same man now. He was working with Tess. That made him his enemy.

"You're John, right?"

Surprised, the barkeep nodded. "John Barnhard."

"How'd you know me when I walked in?"

"Oh, uh, I heard folks greeting you tonight. But I'd have recognized you anyway. Your pa had a tintype of you and your ma. Kept it with him at all times, showing you off to anyone who asked. Sometimes even if they didn't."

Clint slid the bottle out of his way. He was through drinking. "Do me a favor, John. Don't tell me how decent my father was next time I come in, and we'll be friends."

Puzzled, the barkeep agreed. "Uh, okay, Mr. Hayworth."

Clint put out his hand. "It's Clint."

The barkeep wiped his hand before accepting his handshake.

Clint left three-quarters of the bourbon remaining in the bottle. Seemed not even bourbon was enough to dull his senses tonight.

The sun had faded into dusky twilight by the time Tess reached the stream. She paced and waited, wringing out her hands. Tom approached with a look of deep despair in his eyes. Tess noted his usual easy gait now nervous and tense. She went to him and he wrapped her into a grateful embrace. "Tess, thank you. Thank you for coming here. I didn't want to leave Laura for too long. I didn't know who else to talk to about this. And I didn't want anyone to overhear about Laura. You know how some might gossip."

"What is it, Tom?" Tess had a dozen questions for him and she didn't know if she could stand another second of not knowing. Her stomach clamped tight. "Tell me." She pulled out of his arms and looked into his eyes.

"Laura's not herself. I've been patient with her, Tess. Just like you told me. But something's not right. She cries all the time. She doesn't want to hold Abby unless it's to feed her. I left Abby sleeping at Lorilee Benjamin's home. She had a baby months ago and agreed to watch her for me for a little while."

"Oh, no. Laura was so thrilled about the baby. But she was also frightened about being a mother."

"The doctor said those fears are normal, but once a woman has the baby, motherly instincts take hold. He doesn't think there's anything wrong with Laura physically. She's been examined."

"You say she's crying?"

"All the time, Tess. When she's not, she's so moody I can barely say anything to her. I don't know what to do."

"Do you want me to speak with her?"

"That's the problem. It will upset her if she knew I came to you."

"We won't tell her that's the reason for my visit."

"Do you think you can help her?"

Tess didn't want to give Tom false hope. She wasn't any sort of professional, but she'd heard of this happening before. "I knew a woman once, a neighbor, who went through this very thing after giving birth. She spent a lot of time crying for no reason. She couldn't help it and she didn't know why she was doing it."

"That's exactly what's happening. My wife just cries, and when I ask her why or how I can help, she gets even more distressed. The doctor says to make sure she rests and eats properly. I'm doing the best I can."

Tess witnessed Tom's frustration. She set her hand atop his and reassured him the best she could. "I'll try to talk to her, Tom. I'll come by tomorrow. How's that?"

"I can't thank you enough. I'm just so—"

"Confused? Worried? Hurt? This isn't a betrayal on Laura's part, I'm sure. She probably can't help it. I know she loves you and Abby more than anything."

He threw his hands up in a hopeless gesture. "She doesn't even want to hold Abby much anymore."

Tess cringed at the thought. That wasn't like Laura, but she was certain that her friend couldn't control these emotions. At least she'd try to find out if that were true. "I'll talk to her. I promise. I'll do whatever I can to help."

Tom bent to kiss her cheek. "Thank you, Tess. Thank you. I don't know where else to turn. Laura places a good deal of trust in you. And so do I."

"I'll do my best for all of you, Tom."

He looked at Maple, grazing on a patch of grass. "You rode out here all alone?" he said, setting his expression in worry. "The least I can do is escort you back home."

"No, Tom. It's not necessary. Maple knows the way, and you need to get Abby and take her back home."

"Are you sure?"

"I'm sure. The ranch is only a few miles out. I'll be fine."

Tess left the stream and rode home, her mind in turmoil. The irony struck her. Laura had the gift of a sweet child and a wonderful man like Tom who loved her, yet she was unhappy and probably didn't know why. Tess would give anything to be in that position, to have a man love her beyond reason and to bring his baby into the world.

Her concern over Laura put her in a melancholy mood. Once she entered the house, she climbed the stairs slowly and opened her bedroom door.

"Nice of you to come home tonight."

She gasped. Clint stood by her bedroom window, his face shadowed by moonlight. She would have fainted from fright if she hadn't immediately recognized his deep, compelling voice and the outline of his hard, strong body. "You frightened me. What are you doing in here?"

Traces of a smile emerged on his lips. "Waiting for you." He approached her slowly. "And now the wait is over."

Chapter Eleven

There was a look in Clint's eyes that thrilled her. She'd come into this room downhearted with concern over her friend and feeling slightly sorry for herself. It wasn't a notion she would entertain for long. She abhorred self-pity, but in weaker moments she would succumb.

Clint, with just one long, lingering look, had wiped those sensations away. As he came closer, the air grew thick with the scent of bourbon and tall, handsome man. Her heart welcomed him. She didn't want to be alone right now, but propriety set in. She moved to the lamp and turned it up, putting a soft glow in the room. "You shouldn't be in my room."

She bit her lower lip, wishing she hadn't turned on the lamp at all. She had a clear view of his face now and the winning quick smile that set her nerves to jumping.

"You want me here."

How did he know? How in heaven did Clint know

that the fight had gone out of her tonight? In her most honest moments she could admit that she'd been disillusioned after speaking with Tom. She'd always looked to Laura and Tom as the perfect pair. They shared a close, loving relationship. They had a new baby. They adored each other.

And yet they were troubled.

Tess's life had been less than glorious. She looked to Laura and Tom for affirmation that life could be wonderful. In them, Tess had found a measure of hope.

She closed her eyes briefly, then opened them to stare at Clint. The gleam in his eyes grew bright, and she read danger and pleasure and fulfillment in that one look.

Oh, yes. Yes. She wanted that. Tonight. Just once.

Clint tossed his hat on the bed. He removed his gun belt—something he'd begun wearing lately—and dropped it to the floor. "Your turn," he whispered.

A mixture of fear and desire coursed through her body. She shivered and the fear won out. She spun around and put her hand on the doorknob. Clint came up behind her. He pressed his body to hers, his chest against her back, and covered her hand with his over the knob. "Turn around, Tess," he said quietly, nipping at one side of her neck. His moist kisses drew her breaths up short. "Face me, honey."

"We can't…do this," she managed to whisper.

Clint slid his hands to her waist and gently, inch by inch rode them up farther along the sides of her upper body until he teased the undersides of her breasts.

She ached for his touch. Hot, hungry heat burst forth, and her breasts swelled, the tips growing erect and more sensitive.

"Don't fight it, Tess," he said.

She had fought it for days and weeks. She had no fight left in her. Not tonight. She wanted Clint to hold her, kiss her, make her feel like a desirable woman.

He waited. Patiently. Giving her time to make up her mind. If she said no, he would accept it. She trusted in that. But she couldn't say no. She couldn't fight her desire any longer.

She had fallen in love with Clint.

It was impossible. They had no future. She could never trust him with the truth of her identity. She'd lived a violent life. She'd killed. That horrible day hung over her like an ominous cloud.

Clint would never understand. He hadn't yet softened from age and illness. He still had a view of the world as it *should* be and not as it truly is.

Tess turned in his arms. She faced him. His eyes blazed with promise and pleasure and hunger.

He brought his lips down, and the instant their mouths touched flames ignited. His mouth moved over hers in a devouring kiss that shot tingles up and down her body. She quaked from his raw, elemental need.

He kissed her again and again, stroking his tongue, delving deep, exploring in an openmouthed, moist, hot union.

Tess grew warm all over. She burned. The sensations swept through her like a raging fire. She wasn't frightened of him. Though his passion flared, he was gentle and tender in ways that she was just learning.

He skimmed his mouth to her throat, pressing moist kisses, working his way lower, his hands holding her steady at the waist, her back to the door, his manhood rubbing against her riding skirt. The burning intensified. Her need grew stronger.

He slipped his mouth farther and wet the material of her blouse. Her breasts strained through the fabric to feel him and she arched her back.

Tess moaned with tiny sounds escaping her throat, wanting more.

Clint responded. He tried unbuttoning the tiny pearls that fastened her blouse. His large fingers fumbling, he gave up in seconds and ripped the blouse down the center. Pearl buttons flew through the air.

She smiled, and when she caught his gaze, he did, too, and then kissed away her amusement, bringing her back into a mindless swarm of pleasure.

He undressed her, peeling away one piece of clothing after another, his gaze lingering on her as he tossed her clothes aside.

"You're mine tonight, Tess." He lifted her up and carried her to the bed.

Tess reached up for him, but he didn't come to her right away. He stood over the bed, looking at her, his gaze flowing over her body, surveying her from the top of her head all the way to her toes. She was exposed to him. Fully. Completely.

"There's no escaping this," he said.

It wasn't a threat but a statement of fact. He was right. From the moment they'd met it seemed they were meant to come to this juncture in their lives.

"I'm not running anymore," she breathed out.

He gobbled her up with a look. "You wouldn't get far."

Clint removed his shirt, his muscles flexing. There was such strength to him, such manly power, his shoulders so broad, the expanse of his chest so solid.

He had chiseled features, more defined now as all parts of him tightened with need. While Tess softened everywhere, her body melting into a puddle of anticipation, Clint seemed to harden, his jaw clenching, his chest contracting, his whole body rigid.

He kept his pants on but removed his belt before coming to her, covering his body over hers. With arms braced on the bed at the sides of her head, he took her in a long, delicious openmouthed kiss that coiled the pit of her stomach and released a furnace of heat.

She kissed him back with little regard for decency. She was on her back. Naked. Allowing liberties with a man who was her enemy. It didn't matter. She wouldn't deny them this time together. This consuming passion. She would finally fulfill the wonders in her mind with the man she loved.

He touched every part of her, making her wild and wanton and bold. She gave herself up to him, unable to imagine permitting anyone but Clint these freedoms.

His tongue stroked.

Her body flamed.

His hands roamed.

Her heart pounded.

He demanded.

She responded.

His heat…

Became her heat.

He touched the junction of her legs, and the soft, moist folds opened for him when she spread her thighs.

"You're ready for me," he whispered in her ear, his breathing hard.

He continued to stroke her. She squirmed with unexpected tortured delight. "Clint!"

The need in her was strong. Her body moved in gyrations that met and matched his, movement to movement.

"But I'm not ready for you. I've waited too long for this." He moved down her body and came to his knees, lifting her up and mouthing her where his fingers had been seconds ago.

She moaned. Exquisite sensations rippled though her. The position excited her. The things Clint did to her made her cry out in pleasured moans of ecstasy. She lost control of her body.

Clint lifted up to watch her. His fingers replacing his mouth, he stroked her thoroughly over and over. Their eyes met, his gleaming with dark, unbridled pleasure. Her hips bucked again and again, and she felt herself pull up, rein in, and everything went tight.

"Let it go," he said.

The release came with force. She cried out as she convulsed, her senses reeling, absorbing this new feeling. Her body surrendered to the intense pleasure and slowly let down, bringing her back to reality as she gazed steadily into Clint's face.

"Don't think I've seen anything so damn thrilling in my life. I'm about ready to burst."

And Clint came to her then, his eyes hooded, his breaths labored, his restraint defeated.

Clint wanted her wild and wanton. She hadn't disappointed. He'd watched her come to the brink, her expression filled with awe, her sensual, undulating release enough to stir any man's blood and make him crazy with need.

She looked at him expectantly and he assured her with a deep, lusty kiss. "There's more."

Much more.

Tess reached for him and scorched his chest with her touch. Her fingers rode over his skin. "What should I do?"

"You're doing it," he said, lifting off the bed to quickly discard the rest of his clothes.

There wasn't time for her touches. Clint had applied all his willpower into making her ready. Now *he* was ready and his need stood at full mast.

He covered her with his body once again and kissed her lips.

God, how he'd waited for this.

He pushed aside her deceit, letting his desire for her overcome his need for vengeance.

He wanted her. Was dying to be inside her.

He rubbed the tip of his arousal to her and she arched. She was hot and wet, and Clint couldn't take another moment without joining with her. He pushed inside with a solid thrust and met with a barrier.

Momentarily puzzled, he pushed again and the obstacle gave way. He felt the rip, a tearing of Tess's female protection. Liquid spilled over his sex. This was the last thing he'd expected. He'd never lain with a virgin before.

He stared into Tess's sex-hazy eyes, puzzled. His mind raced.

She reached up and pulled him down on her, kissing him soundly. "Don't stop, Clint." She moved her hips and spread wider for him. "I want you."

Nothing could stop him from taking her, but she'd damn well surprised him. He thrust gentler now, moving slowly, building the pressure and watching her. She accepted him, her expression beckoning his movements, and soon she was undulating under him, meeting his thrusts and arching her hips.

Her hair spilled over the pillow, a coppery glow of untamed strands surrounding her face and shoulders. Her skin shone like fresh cream, soft and white. Her arms were positioned up and around her head. The sensual vision she made marked him for life.

He thumbed one rosy, erect bud and saw the pleasure on her face. She sighed and closed her eyes, and he continued to fondle her, working them both up to a frenzied state of arousal.

When Clint couldn't hold back another second, he lifted her hips and thrust harder, deeper, taking them both to heaven with sighs of completion.

When he looked at her sated face, something broke apart inside his heart. He gathered her up into his arms, nuzzled her neck and whispered soft words into her long fall of wavy hair.

She had some explaining to do. But not tonight. Not now. All he wanted to do was keep her close and hold her. She'd given him something precious. He didn't understand why. She was a puzzle he couldn't figure. But he knew he wanted to protect her.

Sunrise dawned with an early ray streaming into the bedroom, waking Clint. He found Tess in his arms, her supple back pressing his chest. He settled in and drew her closer, his hand caressing her soft bare thigh. He roamed higher, over her hip, and she let out a little sound.

He smiled and kissed her throat, pushing her hair aside with his chin. Those waves tickled his face. He grazed his cheek to hers, gently kissing her again.

She murmured incoherent words and turned in his arms. Then she opened those beautiful blue eyes. She lay naked with him, and her first instinct was to pull away.

But Clint coaxed her back with another kiss. "Morning."

She recovered, remembering. She smiled with her eyes. "Good morning."

"Did I hurt you last night?"

"No…you didn't." She closed her eyes. "It was more than I expected."

Clint chuckled. "That's good to hear."

She rolled onto her back and sighed. "I suppose you—"

He came over her to put a finger to her lips, cutting off her words. Then he removed his finger and stared into her eyes. "Not now."

He lowered his mouth, taking her in a long sweep of a kiss. He didn't want her explanations yet. His body wasn't nearly sated. He hadn't roused her from sleep to *talk.*

Waking with her in his arms, crushed to his chest, naked and beautiful, was more temptation than he could possibly fight. She tested his will-power time and again.

He wanted more.

He kissed her again and wrapped both arms around her, coaxing her to roll toward him. Then he lifted her so that her sweet, shapely body covered his.

Making love to Tess in the morning's light equaled that of taking her during the night. She was a striking sight, her breasts firm and lifted, the rosy tips erect. Her body full and giving and so perfect, he couldn't take his eyes off her.

He guided her carefully over him and showed her

how to move, to take him in entirely, squeezing him with a sheath that turned his insides out.

They came together and broke apart together.

And then they fell asleep.

Together.

Tess woke in a dreamy state. She sensed the time was late and she was alone in the bed. With eyes still closed, she recalled the night of fiery passion with Clint. She'd given herself to him and it had been wonderful. Her body still tingled in private places. Tenderness between her legs brought images of Clint and the way he'd taken her, made love to her, taught her things she'd never dreamed were possible to do.

She felt thoroughly ravaged and yet whole at the same time. She wanted to feel that way again.

She smiled.

"That smile have something to do with last night?"

She snapped her eyes open. Clint sat in a chair facing her, his chest bare, his pants on but unfastened and his legs sprawled out lazily. Had he been watching her sleep?

"Maybe," she said, sliding the sheet farther up to her shoulders.

Clint leaned forward. "You slept well?"

"Very well."

She blushed. The conversation seemed odd and too polite for two people who'd done the things they'd done to each other. The memory of how she'd behaved stunned her, but it had felt so right and, strangely, so pure. She wouldn't change one second of being with Clint last night.

Clint drew in a deep breath. His gaze flowed over her as if recalling their passionate night, as well, then his expression changed and his eyes grew pensive. He leaned forward, bracing his forearms on his knees.

He was a beautiful man. He'd been hers last night. But now Tess knew he wanted answers.

"Are you gonna make me ask?" He spoke quietly.

"No."

"You surprised me. I don't usually get caught off guard."

"I, uh…well, I've never been with a man before."

He squinted and looked at the sheet that covered her as if trying to see through it. "That much I know."

"I didn't have…we didn't…well, my relationship with Hoyt wasn't like that. He was my friend. Funny thing about your father—I was supposed to be taking caring of him, and all the while he'd been taking care of me. Helping me. I did love him, Clint. He was the kindest man I'd ever known."

"Spare me," he said, his mouth curving into that scowl that seemed to be ever-present on his face. "Why'd you marry him?"

"I told you—I loved him."

Clint's brows rose. He wanted more of an answer.

"He was dying. We both knew it. He was confined to bed. He wanted me with him most of the time. He insisted on marrying me—for my sake. He didn't want anyone disparaging my reputation, but he said he would have anyway. He really cared for me."

"Maybe he wanted to show everyone he could still bed a beautiful young woman."

Tess shook her head. Clint's bitterness wouldn't allow him to see the truth. The night she'd spent with him had been glorious, and she'd hoped to continue on today with a fresh start. This morning she'd hoped to find the tender, amorous man she'd been with last night, but the day was proving to be no different than any other day since Clint's arrival. He held on to his anger even after she told him the truth about her relationship with his father. "No matter what I say about him, you won't believe me, will you?"

"Doubtful."

Tess stared at him and sighed. "Then there isn't much more to talk about." She grabbed the sheet tighter to her chest. "Will you leave so I can dress? I have to go into town today and I'm already late."

Clint rose. His scowl deepened. "Are you meeting with Tom Larson again? Is that why you're rushing off?"

Tess's mind spun. She blinked. "T-Tom? You know?"

Clint fastened his trousers, eyeing her with suspicion. "I know you met with him last night."

Tess wrapped the sheet around her and bounded from the bed, glaring at him with her own suspicions. "How do you know that?"

"I followed you."

Her mouth gaped open. She couldn't believe it.

"I found your note. You met him in your *secret* place."

"You *followed* me?" she asked, her voice elevating.

"Damn right I followed you. There's been so much going on around here, I needed to find out the truth."

Once the shock wore off, her blood heated and she trembled in anger. "And what did you find out?"

Clint buckled his trousers with a tight pull on the strap. He cast her a narrow-eyed look. "I saw the two of you meeting together behind Laura's back. That's *enough,* isn't it? I sure didn't expect that…of Tom."

Her hands fisted into tight balls of energy. She looked at him now, hating him for the implication. He suspected her of dallying with her best friend's husband. "You've called me many things, Clint, but I've never been more insulted than at this very moment."

"Tell me why, Tess. Are you behind the accidents here? Is Tom helping you?"

Fury built quickly, her love for Clint Hayworth dissolving like snow on a sunny day. Her heart shattered at his wicked accusations. "You bastard! I will *not* explain myself to you! That's all I've been doing since you arrived here. You came to my room last night and now I know why! You used me. You turned something special into something calculated and cruel."

Tess had been duped and deceived by a master. He'd come seeking revenge. He'd come because he didn't trust her. All softness toward him left her. She knew the true reason for his seduction. He'd taken her body and he'd taken her heart. Well, she surely could take her heart back. And he'd never touch her body again.

He ground his teeth. "Do you deny being involved with Tom Larson?"

Tess refused him an answer. She owed Clint nothing. "Get out!"

He took hold of her arm. She flinched and backed away.

"I didn't hurt you," he said, looking at her arm.

"Oh...yes," she said, holding back tears. "You did." Not by his gentle grasp but by his coldhearted accusations. He'd suspected her of horrible things and had made love to her only to extract payback. "Now go."

She strode to the door with as much pride as she could muster, holding her chin up. She opened the door and waited.

He grabbed his boots, his gun belt and the rest of his clothes and left, slamming the door behind him.

"I was only a little bit in love with you," she whispered, trying to convince herself that it was true.

And, sadly, not succeeding.

Chapter Twelve

Clint exited Tess's bedroom, jealousy knotting in the pit of his stomach. She'd been a virgin, offering Clint something she'd waited twenty-one years to give. So what the hell had she been doing in a secret meeting with Tom Larson? All he'd wanted was for her to deny his accusations and come clean. He'd wanted her to say the words. He'd wanted to hear her explanation.

Instead she'd gotten her feathers in a ruffle.

He turned on the landing, with clothes in hand, and locked gazes with Greta as she glanced up from the base of the stairs with knowing eyes. A witness to his state of undress, the corner of her mouth quirked up before she continued down the hallway.

Clint dressed with haste and headed downstairs. It was late and all the other hands were already busy at work. In no time he had eaten breakfast, saddled up and mounted Midnight.

He rode fence, checking the barbed wires, righting posts and clearing his head. The sun beat down mercilessly, his hatband soaking up his sweat already, and he hadn't been outside for more than an hour this morning.

The land was dry, the breeze in short supply. He had stopped to sip from his canteen when Randy raced up, bouncing off his saddle.

"Mr. Hayworth," he said, breathing rapidly. "I found ten yards of fence down. I'm sure cattle are missing. Don't quite know how many yet. Some of the crew sent me down to tell you. Looks like someone cut the wires."

Clint handed Randy his canteen. "Take a drink. Catch your breath." He waited for Randy to drink up, then questioned him further. "Did anyone see anything?"

"No, sir."

"Are you sure?"

"I'm sure. The boys were all surprised. They'd come up this way yesterday looking for a new mama and her calf and they didn't see any fence broke down."

"How long have they been out here?"

"They've been working since sunup. Came out right after the breakfast call."

"Okay," Clint sighed. "Show me where exactly. I'd better check it out."

"The boys are sure it happened late last night."

"I'm thinking they're right," he said, setting his hat lower on his head as he rode farther into Hayworth land, kicking up dust, assured now that Tess hadn't had anything to do with this.

She'd been with him all night.

The memory wouldn't soon leave him.

But more than that, gut instincts he trusted told him there was someone else behind these occurrences at the Double H. And he wouldn't rest until he found out who was guilty and why they were doing this.

Tess rocked little Abby on her lap gently while she held Laura's hand. They sat together on Laura's parlor sofa, her dear friend teary-eyed. Tess couldn't remember seeing Laura without a smile on her face or her eyes beaming. Laura had always been a comfort. She could always rely on her friend for her sensible mind. She'd admitted to herself Laura's sullen look and attitude disconcerted her.

"I don't know what's come over me, Tess. I love Abby. And poor Tom, I'm sure he's about to wring my neck. I've been so moody and out of sorts."

"Tom's a good man, Laura. He loves you. I'm sure he only wants you to be happy."

"I should be happy! I have a baby. I have a caring husband. I…I don't know what's gotten into me."

Tess sat back and explained about the woman she'd known who had gone through the same thing. She described her neighbor's feelings of desolation and depression, and Laura nodded in full agreement.

"That's how I feel, too. At times I think I don't deserve any of the good things I have."

"Well, I think you deserve everything wonderful, Laura." She set little Abby onto her cradle bed and then reached into her carrying bag and lifted out the pink scallop-edged baby blanket she'd been working on. "If I didn't think so, I wouldn't have stayed up all hours of the night knitting this."

She handed the blanket to Laura.

"Oh, it's so delicate, just like Abby." Tears dripped from Laura's eyes. "You're such a dear friend. And this is beautiful," she said, staring at the blanket with appreciation. "And a good deal of work."

She smiled. "A labor of love."

Laura set the blanket down. "Thank you. For the blanket and for coming to visit me. The doctor says there's nothing wrong with me that he can see."

"I think it's something you have to work through."

"I'm trying."

Tess hugged her. Laura was the closest she'd ever come to having a sister. "I know you are."

"Poor Tom," she said again.

"He loves you, Laura. He'll be patient. I'm sure these feelings will pass soon."

"Do you really think so?"

Tess nodded. "I do. Maybe instead of resting all day, you should get out of the house. Why don't we take Abby outside for a stroll?"

"It's warm out."

"We'll find shade. Come on. Abby will like it, but I think you'll like it, too."

Laura wiped her tear-stained face. "I think I *would*

like it," she said, bolstering up. "Yes, let's take Abby for a stroll."

Tess spent the rest of the morning with Laura and Abby and was gladdened to see Laura smile more and hold her baby in her arms. She left their house after a light lunch and then pointed the buggy toward home.

When she entered the house she nearly bumped into Greta on the threshold. Speaking rapidly in German, she fretted, wringing her hands with a stark look in her eyes.

"Greta, what is it?"

Greta continued speaking in her native tongue.

Tess took hold of her hands and stilled them, peering into the cook's eyes. "I don't understand a word of what you're saying."

Greta caught herself. She took a breath and began speaking more calmly, her English heavily accented. "Pearl Cowper is here. She is hurt. She *wouldt* not rest. She came to see you."

Tess's heart raced with dread. Memories flashed of her childhood. Awful sensations washed over her, recalling witnessing her brother's beaten body after one of her father's tirades. "Where is she?"

Greta gestured toward the kitchen. "She *wouldt* not let me send for the doctor."

"The doctor? How bad is she?" Tess asked, truly alarmed now, rushing toward the kitchen. When she stepped inside, she gasped. "Oh, Pearl."

The woman sat in the kitchen, her arms braced

against the table, holding a wet cloth to her swollen face. Dark purple splotches appeared on her cheeks. She looked weary and old and frightened.

"She is dizzy," Greta said.

"I couldn't let Ralph hit me again." She spoke bravely, but her body trembled.

"We've got to get you into bed."

"No, ma'am. I'll be fine. This ain't the worst I've had."

Tess bit her lower lip. Pearl's voice sounded weak.

"It's just that this time I hit him back. With a hoe at the back of his head. Then I ran. I didn't know where to go, so I came here."

"I'm glad you did."

"He's bound to be madder than a wild dog."

"Would he come here?" Tess asked.

"Lordy, no. Don't think so, being as he works for you and all. But I might have mentioned your name as I was swinging that hoe."

Oh, God. "Might?"

"Sure enough did," she said, cringing with pain when she nodded her head.

Tess closed her eyes. Part of her wanted to rejoice. Pearl wouldn't stand for his mistreatment anymore. She'd stood up for herself. But she couldn't send her back home to him. She knew what kind of greeting she would get upon her return. Pearl was injured and dizzy. Tess saw her struggle to keep from keeling over while trying to be brave.

"You need to rest. Greta will set you up in a

room. You'll stay with us today and get your strength back."

"Don't matter if I do. Once I get back, Ralph's gonna take that hoe to me more times than I can count on my fingers and my toes."

"Greta, help me get Mrs. Cowper to a bedroom." Tess worked with Greta to lift the beaten woman up. "I don't want you to worry about Ralph today. You'll be my guest for as long as it takes."

"Thank you, Mrs. Hayworth," Pearl said, her body so weak that it took both of them to get her up the stairs and into a bed.

Tess watched Greta fuss over Pearl, tucking her in and making her comfortable. Her mind made up, Tess knew there was only one thing to do—and she'd do it today. There was no time to waste.

Ralph and Pearl Cowper lived on a small parcel of land several miles from town, in a small wooden house in obvious need of repair. Boards covered up broken-out windows, and the knotty planks holding a narrow porch together had caved in, leaving gaps where one could catch a toe if not careful. Vegetables grew in a large garden in rows neatly tended, and beyond that, peach and plum trees were showing the last signs of bearing fruit for the season. Clothes hung motionless on a line behind the house, drying easily in the overbearing heat.

Tess pulled the brake on the buggy and stepped down. She looked around for Ralph Cowper. When she didn't find him near the barn or in the yard, she walked over a gaping hole on a plank board leading to the house and knocked. "Mr. Cowper?"

No answer.

"Mr. Cowper, it's Tess Hayworth. I'd like to speak with you." She knocked again, harder. "Mr. Cowper, are you in there?"

Her next thought was that Pearl might have whacked him too hard upside the head. He could be severely injured. Or dead. That would solve Pearl's problem, wouldn't it? If he were dead, Pearl could live a life free of worry and fear.

Tess shouldn't be thinking this way. She shouldn't wish a person dead. Having seen Pearl, though, and known of her abuse from her confessions, Tess had no sympathy in her heart for the man. In her estimation, a man who struck a woman wasn't a man at all.

She had her hand on the handle, ready to push her way through, but it was jerked free when the door opened abruptly.

"What?"

She faced a dreary-looking man with deeply etched wrinkles on his face, the skin above his eyelids hanging over his eyes. He wore an undergarment over his staunch belly that was worn and discolored. She'd never met Ralph Cowper before. He worked at Hayworth Freight and was in charge of loading, unloading and taking inventory.

Holding a bloody cloth to the back of his head, he glowered at her, a look she believed was forever on his face. She wouldn't allow that glower to divert her intentions. "I'm Tess Hayworth."

"I know who you are."

"I'd like to speak with you."

He scratched his chin nervously. Tess knew she had an advantage over him. If she were anyone else, he'd be shooing her off his property. But Hayworth Freight employed him. And she was a Hayworth.

He opened the door wider and walked inside.

Tess followed him in. Immediately she saw Pearl's touches around a charmless room—a lace pillow here and a chipped flower vase there, faded curtains that had once been bright with color. Tess felt another pang of sympathy for the woman who'd tried to make this house a home.

"Say what's on your mind," he said, sitting in a chair. "I've got me one hell of a headache."

"I know."

He shot his eyes up. "You've been planting all those notions in my wife's head with them fancy women's meetings?"

"I don't have to. She knows you're not treating her right. Pearl's a strong woman. She'd have to be to put up with your cruelty all these years."

He dabbed at his head and grimaced. "You come here to insult me?"

He repulsed her. She reminded herself that she was doing this for Pearl. "I came here to speak with you. You have to stop beating your wife. No woman deserves that treatment."

"Did she run to you?" His eyes beaded with building fury. He wasn't listening to her. He wouldn't heed her cautions. Instead he wanted to find out where Pearl was.

"I won't say where Pearl is right now. What I want is your promise not to strike her again. Not to make her life miserable. She's a good woman."

He rose from his seat. "She's making *my* life miserable. She's forever doing things to rile me. I won't promise nothing. That woman is so damn *stupid.* She's—"

"She's not stupid!" Tess screamed. "She's not stupid! Do you hear me?" Then she calmed down, realizing that she defended Pearl for all those times no one had come to her defense. Tess never had the courage to talk back to her father and tell him *she* wasn't stupid.

"You got no right coming here, telling me how to treat my woman. It don't matter that you're the high and mighty widow Hayworth! You got no right, you hear me!"

"I'm trying to help you both. Maybe if you and Pearl attended church on Sundays—"

"Church? Ain't no one forcing me to go to church on Sundays. I had my fill when I was a boy. No, ma'am. You gonna fire me 'cause I don't go to church?"

"Listen, Mr. Cowper. I came here to speak rationally with you!" Her voice rose to an uneven pitch, sounding even to her ears most irrational. "I came here to help. You can't beat on Pearl anymore."

"It ain't none of your business."

"You're gonna kill her one day!"

"Wouldn't be much of a loss!"

Any sense of reason escaped her now. She hauled back and slapped his face as hard as she could.

Then she gasped. "Oh!" She abhorred violence. He'd brought her to the brink. "You are a horrible man."

Without hesitation, he drew his arm across his body, ready to knuckle-slap her, but he stopped abruptly, his palm in midair.

Tess froze in fear. She was that little girl again.

"You touch her and you're a dead man."

Clint walked inside the room, putting his body between hers and Cowper's.

Where had he come from? How did he know she was here? Puzzled and trembling, she watched Cowper lower his striking arm and stare at Clint.

"I suggest you think long and hard about striking a woman ever again." Clint stood protecting her. His stance rigid, his voice menacing, he spoke through tight lips. "You want to keep your job or any job in this town, you'll be civil to your wife. You're lucky I didn't get here a minute later or I'd have made you pay a heavy price for disrespecting Mrs. Hayworth. If you don't like my terms, get out. If you stay, you will never strike your wife again. It's your choice."

"You threatening me?"

Clint smiled without mirth. "You could say that."

"I'm not afraid of you."

Clint eyed him, surveying him closely. "You should be."

He turned on his heel and took Tess's arm. "Let's get out of here."

Once outside, Tess wanted to collapse in his arms. She was ready to, until Clint admonished her. "That was a fool thing to do, coming here alone."

He tied his horse to the back of the buggy and helped her up. Then he got in beside her and took up the reins. He encouraged the horse forward with one word.

"What in hell were you trying to accomplish back there?" His voice was as gruff as it had been when speaking to Ralph Cowper. They headed toward the Double H.

"I had to do something. Who told you where I was? And why'd you come?"

"Greta was worried. When she found you gone, she figured you'd come here. She told me about the ladies you're trying to help. Don't you know you can't change a person's nature? You'll get yourself in a pile of trouble trying."

"You don't understand."

"Try explaining it to me."

"I…" she began, then thought better of it. "I can't."

She couldn't be fully honest with Clint. She didn't trust him. She couldn't forget his deception last night. He knew enough about her already, and if she divulged her past to him, she believed he'd use it against her. He still wanted to destroy the Double H. She couldn't allow that. She couldn't allow him to destroy her, either.

"You're stubborn, Tess. I know you've been hurt in your life. You've got wounds inside. We all do. But you can't go interfering in people's lives."

"Someone's got to help her. That awful man could kill her next time."

How could she explain that helping Pearl and other women realize their worth and that they deserve respect and consideration could also help her deal with her past? She couldn't stand by any longer and allow these women to be abused.

"You really fear for her life?" he asked.

She nodded. "Yes, I do."

Clint looked at her a long moment. "Don't go back there again."

"But what if—"

"I'll deal with Cowper from now on. You concentrate your efforts on seeing to his wife."

"This isn't your fight, Clint."

He shrugged. "Maybe it is, maybe it isn't. But now I'm involved."

He didn't have to be. Why, if he hated the Double H and the town that bore his name, would he get caught up in anything like this? Clearly it wasn't his concern.

She'd softened to him yesterday and during the night even more, but she wouldn't make the same mistake again. He'd hurt her, and the injury would stay with her a long time. His deception made her ache deep inside. She couldn't figure out his motives for what he'd done today, but this time around she wouldn't give him the benefit of her trust.

He reined in the horse and stopped the buggy when they reached the house. He helped her down, and his touch sent sparks flying, but Tess chose to ignore them this time. She wouldn't allow tender feelings for him to sway her judgment.

"Thank you for...well for...being there when I needed help."

His gaze rested on her mouth, and she couldn't miss the hunger in his eyes before he lifted them to hers. "There's one more thing," he said.

Tess drew a deep breath, certain he'd tilt his head to kiss her. She found it amazing and ridiculous that she didn't put distance between them. Instead she gawked back at him, waiting. "What?" she breathed out.

He took a step closer and her heart pounded. She wanted to back away and not allow anything more to happen between them, but it appeared she hadn't the will to do that.

She swallowed. And waited.

He spoke again, and it wasn't what she'd expected at all. "Someone cut down a section of fence. Cattle were stolen. Must have happened during the night."

The night that they'd spent together, making love.

"Oh," she said. She didn't know what disappointed her more—Clint not kissing her or the fact that the crimes were still occurring on the ranch. "Did anyone see anything suspicious?"

"Don't think so. None of the men saw anything. The fence is repaired now, but we'd need a thousand men to guard the acres of Hayworth land to catch him if he wanted to do it again."

"What about tracking the missing cattle?"

"They're long gone by now. Someone could have hurried them along and hidden them before we even discovered them gone. We'll keep an eye out for the brand, but it's—"

"Not the missing cattle so much as who's doing this and why."

"That's right. Missing a hundred head in a herd this size isn't going to break us. But someone's trying to upset the scheme of things here."

"At least you know it's not me."

He snapped his head up and his eyes flashed. He spoke quietly, in a whisper for only her ears. "Yeah, I know where you spent last night."

She blushed, the heat rising to her face instantly. She couldn't look him in the eyes.

"You know it's not me, either."

Did she? Did she truly know anything about Clint Hayworth? He was a puzzle she had yet to solve. She let that statement drop. "Well, I'd better get inside and check on Pearl."

She lifted her skirt and moved toward the house.

"Tess." He'd called her name as a quiet command. She stopped and waited with her head down. "We're not through yet."

She blinked, said nothing and walked up the steps and into the house.

Chapter Thirteen

Clint left Tess to tend to the injured woman in the house. He unhitched the horse from the buggy and took the time he needed to settle his nerves. He hadn't been sure what he'd stumble upon when he'd approached the Cowper homestead, but Greta's urgent warning had played havoc with his imagination.

Ralph Cowper would have known his sorriest day if he'd struck Tess. Clint wouldn't have abided that. He didn't take kindly to any abuse of women, whether verbal, physical or emotional. It was obvious Tess felt a need to champion the cause. But she shouldn't go putting herself into dangerous situations. It was a good thing Clint arrived when he had.

He wondered again who had hurt Tess and why. What were the circumstances that caused such a beauty to marry a man thrice her age? Had she been so badly treated that she only felt safe with a dying man?

Last night he'd savored every moment she'd been

in his arms. Once he'd realized her virginity, he'd been as tender as he knew how to be. He'd wanted to cradle her, protect her and treasure her through the night.

Her taste remained in his mouth. Her scent lingered in his mind. He'd claimed her innocence, and seeing that damnable man lift his arm violently toward her had brought out every protective instinct Clint possessed. He'd been ready to pummel the man into the ground.

He might still.

For the first time Clint found some common ground with his father. Hoyt had wanted to protect Tess. Clint wanted to do the same. The woman brought out tendencies in him that he'd kept closed off. She made them surface, and he'd be damned if he could conceal them any longer.

Tess had gotten under his skin.

But she didn't see eye to eye with him about the future of the Double H. Clint wasn't about to change his mind. And it appeared neither would she.

They'd come to a stalemate.

There was another stubborn creature that needed persuading, as well. He entered the corral and closed the gate. The palomino stood at the far end of the corral. He'd allow Clint entrance, but that was all. Clint knew the signs of wariness. The stallion still didn't trust him. Clint wasn't one to give his trust easily either.

He stood just inside the gate, staring at the horse, speaking softly to him and slowly working his way around the perimeter of the fence, step by step. He'd gotten only five steps around when the palomino reared up and snorted. "Easy now, Sunset. You've got a friend here."

Sunset paced back and forth, watching Clint with keen eyes, making noise and shaking his head in frustration. Clint knew it would take some time. The stallion had a strong temperament. Clint stayed in the corral longer and longer each day, taking one step farther around the perimeter. He made slow movements, touching his hand to his hat, kicking out a boot heel, letting the stallion adjust to his gestures and movements.

Clint had invaded his territory and every day he made slight progress with the horse. Once he'd stayed long enough, he tipped his hat. "See you tomorrow, boy."

Clint walked behind a tree to observe what the palomino did next, but hushed voices coming from behind one of the storage sheds caught his attention. He heard Greta's strong accent and walked a little closer toward the sound.

Then he spotted Sonny. The two were arguing about something, Greta pointing her finger at Sonny, and his face flushed with hot color.

Clint walked up to find two guilty faces looking his way. "Afternoon," he said, darting his gaze from one to the other. "What's the ruckus about?"

Sonny pinched his expression tight. "No ruckus."

Greta's chin went up.

"Sounds to me like an argument. Greta?"

Greta shot Sonny a cold look, then closed off her expression before returning her gaze to Clint. "No argument."

Whatever it was, they weren't saying, but he was damn sure the two of them weren't happy with one another. "When you're through *being polite* to each other, we need to talk," Clint said to Sonny.

"I'm through. We can talk now."

"I will make supper." Greta turned on her heel and stalked off.

Sonny scratched his chin.

"Any news today about the downed fences?"

Sonny shook his head. "No one saw or heard anything."

"That seems to be the case with each one of these crimes."

"Crimes?"

"Stealing cattle, cutting fences, poking holes in water tanks. Don't you think on them as crimes?"

Sonny put his hands in his back pockets and rocked back on his boot heels. "Yeah, I'm…beginning to."

"It's time we got the sheriff involved in this."

Sonny drew a breath. There was a slight flicker in his eyes. "Well, now. Hoyt pretty much liked to keep things that happened on the ranch to himself. He usually figured he could fix just about any problem without involving the law."

"That was my father's problem—he thought he *was* the law."

Clint watched Sonny's reaction. He had a strange sense about this. He had to make a trip into town to get the answers he needed. Something didn't add up around here.

He'd hold off informing the sheriff. Right now he had his own suspicions.

And he hoped he was dead wrong.

Tess climbed the stairs slowly, her mind in turmoil. She had a good deal on her mind. The calamities on the ranch were beginning to frighten her. They were no longer harmless pranks but actual crimes. They'd started out as small things, like missing ranch equipment and mysteriously broken wagon hitches, then they'd escalated to shed fires and cattle theft.

What was next? And how could she protect the ranch from these peculiar criminal actions? For the first time in a long while Tess didn't feel secure on the ranch. She remembered the gunfire that caused her mare to throw her. She'd been injured and frightened from that fall. But these occurrences lately had nothing to do with her directly. They were aimed at upsetting the smooth operation of the ranch.

And they were working.

She still couldn't figure it.

When she reached the guest bedroom where she'd left Pearl earlier, she stopped for a moment to take a breath. Then opened the door.

She'd hoped to find Pearl resting or asleep. Instead

Pearl was up, gazing out the window, a desolate look on her face.

"Are you feeling any better?" she asked.

Pearl turned, her eyes filled with such sorrow that Tess wanted to embrace her.

"I'm doing fine, Mrs. Hayworth. I shouldn'ta come here."

"It's a good thing you did. Never doubt that. I'm here to help." She stated the obvious. "Your face is swollen. Does is hurt?"

She moved away from the window and walked over to her. "I've hurt worse."

Tess took hold of her hands. "Oh, Pearl. That's just it. You don't have to hurt at all."

"I don't plan to anymore, Mrs. Hayworth."

"What does that mean?"

"It means I've decided to leave Ralph." She wiped away tears in the corners of her eyes with the backs of her hands. "I should've done it a long while ago."

Tess pulled out a handkerchief from her pocket and handed it to her. She dabbed at her eyes. "Maybe that's a good thing, Pearl. I went to speak with him today. I think Ralph is a man who won't change. At least he didn't appear to back down when I confronted him."

"Oh, Mrs. Hayworth. I didn't mean to be involving you in this. Did he…he wouldn't dare…he didn't do—"

"No, he didn't. He was rude to me. And he wanted to strike me, but Mr. Hayworth talked him out of that real fast."

Pearl's eyes grew wide with disbelief. "Mr. Hayworth?"

"Yes. He'll deal with Ralph from now on. You shouldn't go back there right now."

"I have to."

"But you just said you planned on leaving him."

"I am. I'm through with Ralph. But, you see, I got me some money hidden in the house. I've been selling fruits and vegetables for a time now. It ain't much but enough for me to get to my sister's farm about a hundred miles from here. I'm real good tending the garden. I can sell my vegetables and help my sister. Connie's been invitin' me to come, but I was real stubborn, feeling my duty was to stay with Ralph. Pardon me for saying, but there's nothing here for me in Hayworth. Your meetin's helped me see that."

Tess squeezed her hand gently. "Oh, Pearl. I'm sorry to see you go, but it's for the best. I'm glad meeting with me helped you. I understand what you're going through."

"Somehow I knew that you did." Pearl looked at her with newfound understanding.

"I do. I also know you can't go back home."

"But I got to."

"No, you don't. You'll stay here, and tomorrow I'll take you into town and get you some clothes and all the things you need for your trip. We'll find out when there's a rail or stage going toward your sister's place."

Pearl put her head down. "I can't let you do that."

"Pearl, listen to me. You'd be saving me a thousand more worries if you'd let me do this for you. I don't think I could stand by and watch you go back to that house. It'd be worth everything to me if you'd allow me to do this for you."

Tears flowed down Pearl's blistered cheeks. "Mrs. Hayworth, I don't know how to thank you."

Tess put her arms around the woman's shoulders. "You just did, Pearl. You'll stay with us tonight. Greta is fixing up dinner. In the morning we'll go into town and take care of things."

Pearl backed away from Tess to look her in the eyes. "You're giving me so much. I think this is what I always wanted. But I was afraid."

"You've been brave, Pearl. You have nothing to feel ashamed about."

"What about Ralph?"

"You said it yourself once—he can't get much done around the house. He'll finally see what life is like without you."

"You fixin' to fire him?"

"I should. Lord knows I want to." But Tess figured he'd be less of a threat to Pearl if he had a reason to stay in Hayworth. He wouldn't follow her. He wouldn't be able to torment her. He needed his job. "As long as he does his work, he won't be fired."

Pearl seemed satisfied with that. "That's fair."

Ralph didn't deserve Pearl's worry. Nothing he'd done to her had been *fair*. She was a good-hearted, decent woman who had married a cruel man. She'd been innocent. Tess felt certain satisfaction that she was able to help her. Her private meetings had done some good, and she planned to continue on with her new organization to promote women's worth in the world.

"You go back and rest if you want. I'll let you know when dinner is ready."

"Yes. I'll rest now." She hugged Tess shyly and turned toward the bed and sat down. "You're like an angel, Mrs. Hayworth. I don't know what I did to deserve you, but I'll be thanking God every day."

Tears welled in Tess's eyes and she exited the room, relieved for Pearl and glad she'd have a better life now. Yet consuming despair and loneliness swept her up. Tess had no right feeling this way—her life was far better than most but she couldn't fight what was in her heart.

Overwhelming sadness.

"Are you saying that Hoyt didn't provide for Sonny Blackstone and Greta Deutch in his will? Nothing? Those two have worked for my father for over twenty years."

Clint sat in a stitched brown leather chair in David Heaton's office in town, staring at the well-groomed attorney in disbelief.

"That's a fact, Clint. You can look over the will again if you'd like."

Heaton shuffled through files in a cabinet, coming up with Hoyt Hayworth's last will and testament. He fingered through the pages, studying the will and shaking his head. "No. I drew up this will personally with your father at the house. He was bedridden at the time but still sharp as a knife's edge when it came to his business. He provided for you and his wife, split fifty-fifty, as you know. The only other provisions were to charities and his church. He set up a trust for that, and I make sure they receive their sums monthly. That's it."

Heaton slid the papers across the desk, then sat down. Clint took a moment to peruse them before sliding them back. "Hard to believe. Sonny's loyal to the ranch. And Greta, well, she's been like a member of the family."

The attorney stacked his files neatly on the desk. "It's not all that unusual. Many people keep their assets strictly in the family. Your father had a real sense of family, Clint. He wanted to provide for his wife and for you. You two were all he had. You were his main considerations."

Clint disregarded the attorney's statement. He refused to believe his father had cared for him. He'd wanted Clint to continue on with the Double H because even in his death he couldn't bear to have his legacy fail. No, he'd cared more about Hayworth holdings than he had about the son he'd produced or the woman who'd given him that child.

"If I may ask, how is it working out?" Heaton asked, leaning back in his swivel chair. "How are you managing your forced partnership with Mrs. Hayworth?"

"Forced partnership?" Clint had never thought on

it like that. The way Heaton put it and the way he looked at him now with an expectant expression on his face galled the hell out of him. "It's not a partnership at all. I'm planning on buying T—uh, Mrs. Hayworth out. Then I fully intend to sell off parcels of the ranch."

Heaton didn't appear surprised. "I've heard word of your intentions."

"How the hell did you hear about that?"

"Well, uh…" Heaton rose from his seat and stared out the window behind his desk. He had a garden and iron bench seats outside his office. Vines climbed a trellis, and greenery surrounded the area like a private little alcove. The austere room Clint had been ushered into spoke of great wealth with rich furnishings. No doubt his father had paid David Heaton quite handsomely, seeing as Hayworth holdings provided more than half of the town's income. "Let's just say I make it my business to keep informed." He turned from the window. "Your father was a friend, Clint. I've known him for years. He wanted—"

"Don't tell me what a great man he was." Clint rose and put his hat on, lowering the brim. "I've heard it all before. But you didn't know the real Hoyt Hayworth."

"Maybe I did, Clint. Maybe you're just going by a hurt youngster's image of his father. Have you given yourself a chance to know him as the man he was?"

"My father is dead. And what's done is done."

"Are you having any luck convincing his widow to sell?"

Clint took in a quick breath, staring at the attorney.

"She won't. She was loyal to him. Hoyt trusted her."

"We'll see."

"I wish you the best, Clint." He put out his hand. Their business had concluded.

Clint shook his hand. "Thanks for your time. I'll be rendering your services once I get my hands on the other half of the Double H."

Heaton shook his head, looking chagrined, and Clint left his office and headed for home.

He'd found out what he needed to know.

And he hated the road his suspicions had taken him.

Clint exited the barn, keeping an eye out for signs of Sonny or Greta. He'd been dogging them for the past three days. Normally, seeing them in a heated argument, as he had that afternoon, wouldn't have caused him any alarm. Greta had a temper. She was accustomed to things on the ranch running a certain way. The same could be said for Sonny. He was as devoted to the Double H as Hoyt had been. Though Sonny didn't rile easily, when he did, grown men on the spread shuddered. He and Greta had been known to get into it a time or two.

But what got Clint thinking were the guilty looks on their faces and the way they'd clammed right up the minute they'd noticed him approaching. He wished he had concealed himself and listened in on their conversation.

Since then, he'd resorted to walking quietly into a room or listening to conversations before winding around the corner of the house or barn. He hadn't caught them in anything suspicious since that afternoon.

Unexpected thunder blasted in the distance, and Clint lifted his eyes skyward as he walked across the yard to the house. Blue skies gave way to treacherous, fast-approaching gray clouds. That booming sound meant trouble. Clint turned on his heels and ran to the bunkhouse to gather up the few men who weren't out on the range. He burst open the door catching three wranglers resting on their beds, and one playing cards. "Storm's coming," he called out. "Let's get the horses inside."

In a flurry of bunkhouse activity, boots, hats and slickers were tossed on and gun belts fastened. Clint led the men to the corrals. "Get them all in the barn and stables! The storm's gonna be a soaker!"

Clint worked with the men as lightning struck in the distance and thunder boomed again. Rain poured down, the drops fat and hard as they landed on his body.

"We need more lead ropes!" he called out. "They're getting jumpy."

Clint calmed and soothed each skittish horse. He worked his way through the corral, slipping a rope over a horse's head and walking him over to a wrangler before relinquishing the rope.

By the time the last horse was ushered into the barn and stables, everyone was soaked to the bone. "Good job. We got them all."

Flashes of lightning sparked in the dark, gloomy

sky. Clint turned his attention to the horse alone in his own corral.

They'd gotten all but *one*.

Sunset kicked up a big fuss, and Clint wanted to get him out of that corral to safety. He approached the gate and eyed the obstinate creature.

"You gonna get him, Mr. Hayworth?" Randy asked.

"I'm gonna try." He entered the corral holding a looped lasso in his hand. "Keep the gate open a bit and be ready to slam it shut in case this doesn't go well," he told Randy.

Black clouds filled the sky and rain poured down with no letup. Clint walked slowly toward Sunset, rain sliding off his slicker like a waterfall. The horse reared and bucked. "Easy boy," he called out, raising his voice over the thunder and sheets of rain.

Sunset reared up again, frightened and obstinate and angry. Then he charged. With nose down and intent on his purpose, he barreled forward, aiming for Clint.

Clint turned on his heels and ran. "Shut the gate!"

Randy hesitated just long enough for Clint to run out before slamming the gate shut. Both men secured the gate, leaving the frustrated palomino to pace and prance on the other side.

"He's spooked," Randy said. "You almost didn't make it out. He woulda crushed you."

"The storm's not bothering him." Clint eyed the horse, understanding his frustration. "He wasn't after me."

"He wasn't?"

Clint shook his head. "He saw his chance for freedom. He wasn't about to pass it up." Clint placed his arm around the young ranch hand's shoulder. "C'mon. Let's get inside. Sunset'll just have to last out the storm."

Randy nodded and headed for the bunkhouse, and Clint went in the back door of the house. He shook off his rain slicker and hat and left them on a hook in the kitchen to dry before climbing the stairs to his room.

He peered out the window as lightning struck in the distance, illuminating the sky in an eerie blaze of light. Clint glanced down to the corral, wondering how Sunset fared.

"Son of a bitch!"

The palomino was gone, the corral gate open.

He and Randy had secured that gate good and tight just minutes ago.

Clint retraced his steps and donned his hat and slicker quickly. Within minutes he'd saddled up and taken off on Midnight in search of the palomino.

He had no doubt in his mind that someone had deliberately let Sunset out of the corral.

"You're a fool for chasing that stallion in the storm." Tess sat on the edge of Clint's bed, dabbing at his bloodied face none too gently with a cloth.

"You nearly shot me," Clint said, allowing Tess to tend to his wounds, eyes twinkling. He enjoyed this little scene too much, she thought.

He'd nearly been crushed when Midnight lost her

footing in the storm. From his accounting, horse and rider went down together, Clint barely escaping the full impact of his mare's weight.

"You were making enough commotion downstairs for ten men, Clint."

"You could've shot my head off, pointing that gun, calling me out."

"Good thing I recognized you when I did."

"I can't argue with that."

Clint rested back on the bed, his shirt open and hanging loosely from his shoulders, his muscled chest bloodied where he'd been injured. Her heart sped being this close to him again. Her frustration rose, as well, realizing that he could have been crushed under his own horse tonight. Nothing was simple with Clint. He always seemed to evoke a wide array of emotions in her.

He stared at the ceiling. He spoke quietly through tight lips, his controlled anger evident. "Someone let Sunset out of the corral. It was deliberate. I'd just left him and saw to that gate myself. Someone's trying to upset the balance here. They've got you so jumpy you're picking up a weapon to defend yourself."

Tess had known moments of panic when she'd heard those noises downstairs. She'd been worried about the ranch and the acts of sabotage lately. She'd grabbed Hoyt's gun, ready to protect herself, refusing to be caught unaware ever again.

When she'd seen Clint at the base of the stairs, struggling to climb them, she'd taken quick action and helped him to his room. She'd helped him take off his wet shirt, removed his boots and gotten him on the bed.

She couldn't bear seeing him bloodied and banged up. The thought of what might have happened to him frightened her more than any acts of sabotage.

In that moment she knew what he meant to her. She knew how much she cared for him. And her feelings for him only irritated her.

"Well, you should've known better, racing out in that downpour." She dabbed roughly at a gash on his shoulder.

"Ouch!"

She smiled. "Sorry."

He smiled back. "You don't sound sorry."

"And you sound like a baby."

Clint grabbed her hand. She didn't pull away. Their eyes locked in the dim lantern light. Her heart raced. He laced their fingers and tugged her closer. She went willingly, softening to him, remembering her fear when she'd thought him seriously injured.

"I'm a man, Tess." He pulled her closer yet and brought her mouth to his. "Kinda hard not to notice with your hands all over me."

Surprised, she tried to pull away, but he caught her, easily wrapping his arms around her. He kissed her, and whatever fight she had left inside vanished.

She couldn't deny Clint. Not anymore. She loved him.

He brought her over his body, sprawling her atop him, and kissed her again. She felt his need, the length of his hardened shaft pressed between her legs.

There was no mistaking his desire. He'd proven his point and Tess was glad of it.

He drove himself deep into her mouth and continued to kiss her until all the breath swooshed out of her.

"I need you, Tess."

She closed her eyes. She'd never heard those words spoken with such clarity, with such honesty. She'd never believed them more than she did now.

"I need you, too," she whispered.

"Undress for me," he said. "Let me see you."

It all seemed so right. So natural. She set aside her unease and rose from the bed, the hungry gleam in his eyes encouraging her. He rolled onto his side, braced his head in his hand and waited.

The house was quiet but for rain, softer now, pitter-pattering on the roof. Tess could hear her heart beating against her chest. Pounding. Pounding.

She lifted her hand and unfastened one button, then another from the high-neck collar of her dress. When all the buttons were undone, she stood there unsure. Then she mustered her courage, drew a breath and slipped the gown from her shoulders. It fell at her bare feet. She stood in her flimsy chemise, unable to meet his eyes any longer.

Clint lifted from the bed. He faced her, winding his hand around her neck, bringing her close. "Lord, you're still so *innocent*." He kissed her tenderly.

"And beautiful." He pulled pins from her hair. The tresses fell onto her shoulders.

There was something she couldn't fathom about Clint tonight. He was playful and sweet and so unlike the man who'd first barged into her sedate life on the Double H.

He slid the chemise down, and when it caught at her slight hips, he hooked his thumbs and guided it down. She broke out in goose bumps from his gentle, searing touch.

He worked his hands up to her waist and then stepped back, looking into her eyes. "You belong with me."

Tess melted inside. She felt the same. She finally *belonged*. It was what she'd wished for as a young girl. She'd wanted to belong *somewhere* and know that she was cared for. Maybe loved. She'd wanted a place to call home. She dared to hope that she'd have that home now, with Clint.

"Yes, I belong with you," she said softly.

Clint's gaze flowed over her bare body. She witnessed appreciation in his eyes and tenderness as he caressed her with a look. "You're not who I thought you were."

She swallowed. "I know."

He shook his head as if not believing.

Tess touched him, a light feather touch on bruised skin. Then she kissed his chest where her fingers had just been. The pleasured sound he made filled her heart with joy.

He wound his hands in her hair, pressing her to him. He kissed the top of her head, her forehead, and drizzled kisses down her cheeks. He found her mouth and claimed her again in a long, slow, earth-moving kiss that brought hot streams of heat below her waist.

He cupped her derriere and pressed his manhood to the juncture of her legs. Her breasts crushed against his chest. He groaned and lifted her up quickly, setting her carefully on the bed.

She ached for him. She belonged not only *with* him but *to* him. She lifted her gaze and saw raw, un-bridled need in him.

He lowered himself down and brought them both...*home*.

Chapter Fourteen

Clint liked waking up with Tess in his arms. She lay curled up against him, her sweet-smelling hair fanning over his chest. Mornings like these were rare. Seldom did he ever share the morning with a woman.

It was different with Tess. He couldn't get her out of his mind. She was standing in the way of what he wanted most in life—to settle an old score with his father. He should resent her.

Actually, he had. When he'd first stepped foot on the Double H after a ten-year absence, he'd held nothing but bitterness and resentment toward her. He'd been certain she was a happy widow, relishing her newfound lavish life and glad the old man was dead. She had power now and more money than any man in the entire state of Texas.

She had it all.

Or so he'd thought. Then he'd seen her in the meadow giving her full attention to Laura's baby, cuddling the child to her chest, holding her with loving arms. He'd seen her kindness for Pearl, a near stranger, and her outrage at Pearl's cruel husband, Ralph. He'd learned of those women's meetings she insisted upon having, and even though he thought her efforts futile, he had to admire her gumption for trying.

She wasn't a woman who settled. She seemed to want to change things…for the better.

Clint winced at the thought.

Was *he* one of the things she wanted to change?

When she stirred and made little throaty sounds, Clint smiled, grateful for the distraction. He wouldn't think about Tess's motives any longer.

"Morning, honey," he said, lifting her hair to kiss her long, slender neck.

She purred like a kitten and rolled over to face him, her eyes sparkling. "Clint," she said lazily, "is it morning already?"

He nodded, enjoying the crush of her generous breasts against his chest. "The birds are catching worms."

She gazed into his eyes, biting on her lip. "We should get up. I should go back to my room. What must Greta think?"

"Greta? There isn't a thing that goes on around here that she doesn't have an opinion on."

Tess pursed her lips into a deep frown. "That's exactly why we shouldn't—"

He kissed away her words. Her lips were warm

and ripe and moist. Clint kissed her again, cupping her head in his hands. "Don't worry about Greta."

"I do worry. She *wouldt* not approve," she said, feigning Greta's deep German accent.

Clint grinned.

"It's just that she disapproved of me marrying Hoyt. She didn't accept me. After he died that didn't change. But I think…that maybe she has accepted me now."

Clint stroked her arm, allowing her softness to seep into his palm. "We have a few minutes before the crew wakes up looking to fill their bellies. I don't want to waste the time talking about Greta, do you?" He pulled the sheet down slowly and looked at her in the morning light, his heart clenching and his need for her strong.

Her face flamed crimson, but she shook her head. "No," she said. "Let's not talk at all."

She rolled over and lay on the bed, waiting for him, her expression shy. Every nerve in his body went still. He'd never seen anything more beautiful or wanted anything more. Clint covered his body over hers. She reached up and brought him down to kiss his lips, her hands wrapping around his neck, her fingers thrust in his hair.

Her passionate responses created an essential need within him. He had to have this woman. She'd reached deep inside and touched him in ways he would have never fathomed. There was a certain innocence about her. How could he have missed it? How could he have been so damn wrong about her?

Now all he wanted was to make up for lost time and take this to wherever it would lead them.

There was no time for the slow, steady, torturous buildup of desire. He'd taken her twice during the night. Her body was attuned to his. He knew her now and she knew him. She was ready to accept him.

He urged his shaft into her, driving deep, and his low guttural groan of their joining was more than pleasure and need. Raw emotion and powerful senses slid over him. The impact stunned him. His thrusts fiery and his demand great, he plunged inside. She took him in fully, gazing at him with clear blue eyes, and breathed his name in an urgent whisper. *"Clint."*

Nothing in his life had ever been this good. This innocent. This sweet.

She renewed him and made him whole again.

Tess Morgan Hayworth. The last woman he'd have thought could ever affect him this way. She rained on his fiery existence and washed away every last remaining burning ember.

He moved with her, fast and furiously. The bed creaked and the mattress bounced. Tess took his thrusts, arching up and rising to meet him. She moaned with satisfied sounds. Her completion came with hard, tight spasms of release.

"Tess!" He couldn't hold back another second. He lifted her hips and spilled into her, claiming her again and again with untamed, feral force. His climax came powerfully, a wild drive of completion.

With his body sated, his heart racing, he lowered

down and kissed her, stroking through her hair, whispering his pleasure, still deep inside her.

She accommodated him so naturally. She fit him perfectly. Clint reveled in the gift she'd given him. He still couldn't believe his good fortune, coming back here, meeting her and, for once, seeing his future clearly.

With Tess in it.

He rolled off her and lay by her side. Massaging her silken skin absently, he thought he'd like to wake up every morning this way. "Wish I didn't have to get up."

"Mmm." She rested her head on his shoulder. She was spent and sated and he wanted to keep her that way. "You're not going after that stallion again, are you?"

Clint didn't want the reminder of what had occurred last night to mar this waking time. Nothing had been settled. There was still a threat out there, and whoever was guilty wasn't letting up. "No, I think the palomino is long gone. Only horse I couldn't tame."

"You told me people don't change their nature. Maybe that's true of some animals, too."

He stroked her arm, both of them gazing at the ceiling. "I hadn't come across a one yet that didn't respond to me."

"Maybe you're losing your touch," she said, teasing.

He looked into her smiling face. "If you think that, give me a minute. I'll prove you wrong."

She shoved the pillow in his face and laughed, a sound he rarely heard. "Oops! Sorry, Clint."

He pushed the pillow away and grinned. "You little tease."

"There'll be no more proving anything today. I've got to get dressed."

She rose from the bed, but he grabbed her wrist before she could get away. She landed on the bed on her knees, blessedly naked before him. She'd gotten over her shyness with him. He sucked in a breath. "Where do you think you're going?"

"Into town."

"Oh, yeah?" He slid a finger down the valley between her breasts. Her nipples hardened. "Bet I could make you change your mind."

She gazed down at him with a tilt of her head. "Maybe you'd like to come with me?"

Hell, he didn't want to spend a minute in or out of his bed without her. "Why would I do that?"

She shrugged and took both of his hands in hers, her eyes intent on his. "We're having a little memorial for…Hoyt today. At the cemetery."

Clint dropped her hands and shook his head in disbelief. The irony struck him. He'd bedded his father's widow last night. He was probably falling in love with her even though she stood in the way of his plans. He still didn't want any part of the ranch. He wanted no part of Hayworth holdings. He had a home in Houston. He had etched out a good life there.

But he wanted Tess. He'd planned on convincing her to sell him the ranch, break up the empire and leave with him. Did she think he'd change his mind because of their hot, passionate nights together? He'd once believed that about her but no longer. She wasn't the conniving bitch he'd once thought she was. And even though he trusted her now, he wouldn't change his mind about his father. "Why?"

She pulled the sheet from the bed and covered herself. "The headstone just arrived. A few of us thought the memorial would be a nice way to say a final goodbye."

"I said my final words to him ten years ago."

She didn't argue the point, which surprised him. "I understand." Despite her words, she registered disappointment, her lips pursing into a little pout. She dressed quickly and left the room.

Leaving Clint alone to stew on his conflicting thoughts.

Clint stood in the shadows behind a tree, quite a distance from the memorial service held on the slope above the plot of land designated solely for Hayworth family members. The headstone was large, detailed with bronzed lettering, with room enough for added names of family members when the time came.

His mother's name held no place there. And Clint would hold no place there. It could very well be that Hoyt would be the only name on that headstone for eternity. His plans for a Hayworth legacy wouldn't come to pass. Clint took some solace in that.

Dressed in black, Tess took her place on the rise. The "few" she'd spoken about had turned out to be almost half the residents of Hayworth, as well as Sonny, Randy and few ranch hands who weren't on duty this morning. He listened to a dozen townsfolk say their piece about Hoyt.

One man stepped up. "Mr. Hayworth gave me a chance when I first came to this town. I promised him a hard day's work and I delivered. He would come to me and say he was proud of my dedication. I'll never forget his generosity."

Then another said, "When my girl took ill with the fever, Mr. Hayworth saw to her doctoring." A young girl set a batch of wildflowers on his grave and said a prayer. "My Jenny is fifteen now and doing good."

"He wasn't an easy man to know. He was a fierce competitor," one of the local ranchers added, "but we respected each other. He was fair, and that's saying something since he owned almost every business in this town."

Sonny came forward next, speaking of his employer Hoyt, who had become his very close friend over the years. He spoke of his mother, Melody, of Clint and then about the years Hoyt had sacrificed building the Double H and the town of Hayworth. "He was hard-nosed at times, with the determination of ten men. He was fair to most. He tried real hard to be a good man. He loved this town. He loved his ranch. He loved his family, most of all. He once told me everything he did was so his family would have something solid to hold on to once he was gone." Sonny teared up a bit. "Hoyt and I grew old together.

He and I, we had our share of disagreements, but I'm proud to say he was my best friend." Sonny stepped away on shaky legs.

Clint watched and listened, his nerves grating. He disregarded everything Sonny had to say, placing no credence in his teary-eyed statements. Sonny had been a loyal employee and had helped build the empire in the early days, but his father had made no provisions for him in his will. Now Clint wasn't sure about Sonny's true intentions.

Clint surmised the people at the memorial were all beholden to Hoyt in some way. They'd come to make a show before his widow. They'd come to butter her up. He knew for a fact that Tobias Lockhurst, the rancher making his claims, had had dealings with Hoyt and secretly despised him. The others, too, had something to gain by being here.

Clint couldn't abide this service or the need for the memorial. When the testimonials ended, Tess stepped up, speaking softly. He strained to hear her.

"Thank you all for coming to this little service. Hoyt would have appreciated knowing you held him in high regard. As his wife, I can tell you I didn't know a more decent, respectable man. He was a dear person, a fair businessman and a generous man. He was my friend as well as my husband. But I will say that Hoyt was often misunderstood. As he grew older he sought to clarify misconceptions surrounding him. Yes, he'd made mistakes, but I haven't yet met a person who has not, at least once, made a bad decision. Hoyt will always hold a special place in my heart. I will always think of him fondly, with love."

Clint ground his teeth. Tess's admission, her undying words of admiration for his father, made his blood boil. He'd only come to keep a watchful eye on her. Too much had happened on the ranch lately. Though he'd convinced her otherwise, he wasn't entirely sure Ralph Cowper would heed his warnings from the other day. Men that desperate often reacted rashly.

Clint wasn't about to let Tess go into town by herself today. This time he hadn't followed her out of suspicion or jealousy. She must have had a good reason for meeting with Tom Larson that day, though she hadn't spoken of it and he hadn't asked again. But he sure as hell couldn't stand by her side and listen to the claims of loyalty to his father.

He'd come here only to see to her safety.

After the memorial ceremony, Tess stayed on a bit to lay flowers on Hoyt's gravesite. To speak to him silently. To pray that Clint would cease his vendetta and come to live at the ranch peaceably.

She walked back to town alone. She thought she'd check in on Laura and hold Abby for a while. She never could get enough of loving that little babe and she prayed Laura's moody bouts had quieted some.

Hayworth thrived. Tess enjoyed seeing the crowded streets, people walking with determined steps to their destinations, storefront neighbors sweeping out their shops and conversing with each other. Cattle pens filled daily with beeves ready to make their way to market. Ranchers crossed the streets for shaves, haircuts and a drink from the saloon.

Often Tess marveled at how one man could have built a town to such rising success. Hoyt had been proud of his business accomplishments, but he'd also been brokenhearted that he'd lost his son's love. Tess ached for both of them and their loss.

Clint was stubborn and prideful and there seemed to be no changing his mind. But she loved him with everything she had inside.

At times she feared her love for him, but after the wonderful night they'd spent together she felt more confident that Clint would come around. He looked at her with tenderness now, and the gleam in his eyes proved more joyful than guarded.

Maybe in time she could ease his pain and bitterness. And maybe he'd give up his plan to destroy the Double H. She held on to that hope as she sashayed down the street.

"Lady, lady," a man called out from the narrow alleyway between the saloon and the dry-goods store. "Help me, help me. It's my leg."

The man was down, curled with pain, grabbing his right knee. She rushed to him and bent. "Oh, dear, what happened?"

In a swift move, he took her shoulders, bounded up, lifting her from her bent position. He jammed her body against the wall.

"Oh!" Startled, Tess lost her bearings for a moment.

"Mrs. Hayworth, is it?" He transformed from a man in agony to one with an ugly snarl on his face and sinister black eyes. "I think *not*. I know who you really are—the bitch who killed her own brother. You're Theresa Metcalf, passing yourself off as a respectable widow."

He grabbed her arm and pulled her farther into the alley. She glanced back for help, but they were encased in dark shadows now and well hidden.

"What do you want?" She'd raised her voice, hoping someone would hear.

He cupped her mouth with his hand. "Shut up and listen!" he hissed under his breath, casting glances down the alley. "Or you'll be sorrier than you know."

He yanked her arm and she cringed with pain. "I want cash. Ten thousand to start. And you'll pay up. Unless you want everyone to know who you really are. You see, I've been biding my time here, checking things out. You passed yourself off as the innocent Miss Tess Morgan from Oklahoma," he said, his voice mockingly sweet. "You nabbed a rich old man. But the deceiving widow Hayworth's gonna make me a rich man now—or else I'll tell the whole town you're nothing but a lying, cheating, murdering whore. What'd they think of the sweet widow Hayworth if they knew that an outlaw's blood runs in your veins? Theresa Metcalf picked up a weapon and shot her brother dead."

Tess shook, her entire body trembling. She struggled, but he had a lock hold on both arms now. "Who—who…are you?" she managed to ask.

"I rode with your brother. I've seen you a time or two with—"

"Let…her…go."

Both turned in the direction of the menacing voice.

Clint came out of the shadows, wielding his gun, his face red with fury.

The man looked at Tess. "Ten thousand," he said before shoving her backward against Clint and rounding the corner of the alley, then disappearing.

Clint grabbed hold of her, keeping her from stumbling. His strength eased her fear and braced her from injury. But when he turned her around, he pinned her down with dark eyes, his expression masked and unreadable. "Is it true?"

Had Clint heard it all? It didn't matter. She was tired of the secrecy. The lies had to end now. She would tell him everything. She closed her eyes and nodded.

"Go to Laura's house. Stay there. I'll be back."

"What are you going—"

But Clint had already taken off, racing down the alley and turning the corner, chasing the blackmailer.

"Be careful," she whispered, crisscrossing her arms to keep her shivers of panic down.

Rusty had ridden with dreadful, ruthless men. Tess prayed for Clint's safety.

Please, God, keep him from harm.

Clint would know the entire truth about her now.

All she could do was go to Laura's house as he'd asked.

And hope he'd return to her.

Tess stood at the Larson front porch on wobbly legs. The blackmailer had frightened her, but Clint's unreadable expression just minutes ago had frightened her even more. She didn't know what Clint was thinking, but he'd said he would come for her, so she clung to that notion. Drawing a steadying breath, she knocked on Laura's door.

She heard soft footsteps, then Laura opened the door, holding little Abby. "Dear Lord," she said after taking one look at her. "What's wrong?"

Tears filled Tess's eyes. She couldn't utter any words.

"Come in," Laura urged, "and tell me what happened."

Tess followed her into the parlor.

"Just let me set Abby into her cradle, she was a bit fuss—"

"No, please, Laura. Let me hold her. I really need to hold her." Tess put out her arms.

Laura stared at her. "Sure." She gestured toward the sofa and Tess sat down. "Aunt Tess wants to hold you," she said to her child softly before carefully handing Abby to her.

Tess took the baby in her arms as tears spilled down her cheeks.

"You're scaring me, Tess." Laura sat beside her,

dabbing at her face with a handkerchief with gentle care. Then she pressed the cloth into Tess's hand.

"I don't mean to." She dried her tears, refusing to give in to them again.

"I know the feeling. I've cried enough tears to fill a rain barrel these past few weeks."

"Are you feeling better?" Tess asked, realizing that her friend had troubles of her own.

Laura spoke honestly. "A little. It's a bit better now. Tom's been a saint, but I'm not quite myself yet."

"I'm so terribly sorry you had to go through this."

Laura *never* told a lie. Laura was an honest, upright person. She hadn't lied her way through her life. She hadn't wielded a gun to shoot and kill her brother. Laura would never deceive the man she loved.

But Theresa Metcalf had done all those things.

And now Clint had gone after a horrible man. If anything happened to him, she'd never forgive herself. She couldn't live knowing her lies could cost Clint his life.

"Oh, Laura," she began, "I'm in love with Clint. Deeply in love."

Laura's face lit with hope. "I'm happy for you."

"I wish I could be happy. It's impossible. An outlaw who rode with Rusty recognized me in town today. He lured me into an alley and tried to blackmail me. Clint heard it all."

"Oh, dear." Laura put her arm around her shoulder. Tess welcomed the comforting touch. "Did he hurt you?"

She'd been shoved against the wall, her arms clamped by his viselike grip, and frightened to death. "Some. But I'm all right. Shaky." She attempted a smile to console her concerned friend.

"I'm terribly worried," she confessed, rocking little Abby and finding comfort in that. "Clint went after him. He had fury in his eyes. I think he was more furious with me than the outlaw. I'm afraid of what he might do."

"Clint can take care of himself. He'll come back for you."

"I'm praying so." She looked at the sleepy baby in her arms and calmed a little. "I've really made a mess of things," she whispered.

"You did what you had to do," Laura reminded her. "You were honest with Hoyt. And I know you'd planned on telling Clint the truth when the time was right."

"I wanted to tell him for a long time now. But I couldn't trust him...he's still so bitter about his father. I didn't think he'd have any forgiveness for me either."

"Tell him that, honey. Tell him what's in your heart."

"I will," she said, determined now. "If he gives me a chance."

Half an hour later, with the baby sleeping comfortably in the cradle, Tess paced back and forth in the parlor as each passing moment Clint hadn't returned brought her dread.

Memories rushed forth of her encounter with Rusty on the last day of his life. Fear, anger and trepidation all came back to haunt her now. Since coming to Hayworth, she hadn't experienced that kind of pure, agonizing alarm. Dismayed, she had the same bad feeling about today.

Laura brought tea and biscuits with her special apricot preserves into the room. She set the tray down. "Sit. Have something to eat."

Tess's hand went to her stomach. Her jittery nerves wouldn't allow her to touch a bite. "Laura, I don't think I can—"

A brisk knock at the door stopped her in midsentence. She froze. Her heart pounded. She stared at Laura.

Her friend smiled. "Sounds like a strong knock. Clint has come for you."

Laura walked to the door, turning to give Tess a nod of encouragement. She opened the door. "Clint, we've been worried about you. Come in."

"No. I won't come in. No disrespect intended. I only came for T-Theresa."

Tess closed her eyes briefly. Clint was all right. She thanked God for that. But he'd asked for her by her given name—Theresa—in a curt, angry tone.

Tess walked to the door to look at him. He held his hat in his hand while speaking to Laura. Still wearing a bruise or two on his face from chasing down the palomino last night, but other than that he looked as handsome and healthy as ever.

Laura turned to give her a hug, whispering, "Tell him, Tess. Everything."

Tess held her embrace for long seconds. "I'll try." She looked at her friend. "Thank you," she said before turning to leave with the man wearing a stony, cold expression.

A man who refused to look at her at all.

Chapter Fifteen

Clint clicked the reins to the buggy she'd left in the field by the cemetery, his horse tied to the back. "Smiley Brown is behind bars."

Thank God. *Smiley,* the man who snarled like a snake and probably would sooner be poked in the eye than cast a genuine smile, had been apprehended.

"Thank you."

"I didn't do it for you."

The quick, hurtful reply only confirmed his obvious anger.

"I'm going back to question him with the marshal after he's had time to stew in that jail cell. He's under suspicion for the crimes on the Double H."

That notion hadn't occurred to her. It gave Clint another reason to be irate. Tess's lies had brought this man here. He'd admitted to being in town for a while, finding out what he could about her and the

Double H. He could very well be behind the disruptions at the ranch.

Tess made several attempts to talk to Clint during the ride back to the ranch, but he cut her off abruptly, refusing her gratitude or her explanations. Knowing his quick temper, she thought it better to give him time to cool down. She held her tongue on the buggy ride home, though she wanted so desperately to explain everything to him now.

Once they arrived, Clint stopped the buggy by the barn and jumped down without casting her so much as a second glance.

Randy rushed up, giving Clint a curious look before helping Tess. "Afternoon, Mrs. Hayworth."

"Hello, Randy." She smiled briefly to the young ranch hand, though everything inside her quaked with sadness and regret. It had been a tumultuous day, filled with heart-wrenching emotions. Although she wished the circumstances were different, Tess was glad the truth was out. Clint was infuriated now, but she hoped to explain everything to him and make him understand why she'd done what she had.

Hoyt had understood. He'd accepted her explanations and helped her become a stronger woman.

But Clint wasn't his father. He may never accept her explanation. Or trust her ever again.

"Can I do anything else for you, Mrs. Hayworth?" Randy asked, his young face filled with question.

"No, thank you," she said softly and turned from him to walk inside the house.

Deflated and fatigued, Tess walked to the staircase and sat on the second step. She put her head in her hands and sobbed quietly. Her tears had flowed at Laura's house, and it seemed now she couldn't hold them back another moment longer.

As a child, crying had been like an addiction to her. Once she began, she had trouble stopping. She'd hide in the corner of her room, hugging her blanket to her chest, and sob until her face was all wet and every drop had been used up. She'd muffle the weeping, fearing her father might hear and come barging into her room.

She didn't want to give in to the tears today. She knew they wouldn't solve her problems, yet she couldn't stop the moisture from pooling in her eyes and dropping down her hot cheeks like a rain shower.

Everything inside poured out of her until she had nothing left. She didn't feel any better. The release had only exhausted her more.

She sniffled and wiped her face with the handkerchief Laura had given her.

The front door slammed. Startled, she snapped to attention.

Clint strode into the foyer and stopped when he spotted her. His face twisted with disgust. "You married my father under false pretenses. By rights, you have no claim to anything Hayworth. Not even the name. I want you off this property. You have until tomorrow."

She rose instantly. "Your father knew the truth about me. I told him everything."

"Can you prove it?"

"You don't believe me?" she asked, indignant.

"Why would I believe anything you say? You've been lying to me since I met you."

"Clint, let me explain."

"No." He shook his head. His gaze burned through her. "I'm not a sick old man like my father. I know who you are now. I won't believe a word coming out of your mouth."

He crossed the foyer to come face-to-face with her, his voice harsh, his expression cold, but there was injury in his eyes. "I wasn't wrong about you when we first met. You're a lying, whoring cheat, an outlaw just like the brother you shot to death."

"Oh!" Appalled at his vicious attack, she stumbled back on the step. She grabbed hold of the banister for support.

"You played the grieving widow really well, *Theresa.*"

"You're wrong about me! I cared about Hoyt. I care…about you!"

"You fooled my father without bedding him, but when I didn't come around, you let me take you. Over and over. And, honey, you were good, so good that—"

"Enough!" Tess had to put a stop to this. She'd heard more than enough. Clint had stunned her with his brutal accusations, but she wasn't a victim anymore. She wouldn't allow his ranting to destroy her. "Don't say another word. I'll leave, but not because you want me gone. I'm leaving because I don't think I can live here with you another second. You're a bitter man, Clint Hayworth, and you think you've never made a mistake. But I'm telling you now you've just made the biggest one of your life."

His eyes flickered for a moment. He drew air into his lungs. Then he whispered, "Just go, Tess. Unless you want the entire town to know who you really are."

"You'd tell them?"

He nodded. "If I have to."

She lifted her chin, turned her back on him and climbed the stairs with determined steps, refusing to show him any more vulnerability. She had a measure of pride left.

Yet deep inside she ached with overpowering regret.

Clint grabbed his gear, saddled up Midnight and rode the mare hard, steering her deep into Hayworth property. He'd ride until he had to make camp at one of the line shacks out on the range. He didn't want to return to the house until the widow was gone. Tomorrow couldn't come soon enough.

Finally he'd come to give Tess his trust. He'd come to think he'd been dead wrong about her. But she wasn't the woman she'd claimed to be. He couldn't abide her deceit and lies.

He'd fallen in love with her.

And she'd betrayed him.

He'd been a fool once again. He doubted the anger and pain he experienced would ebb anytime soon. There was nothing she could say or do to convince him of her innocence. She'd manipulated every situation. He'd been taken in by a willing female with big blue eyes and a body that made him ache just looking at her. She'd been clever, playing the innocent, bedding him and giving up her virginity to gain her end. She'd managed to dupe him into believing she was who she claimed to be.

Clint pressed Midnight to race faster. He bent low in the saddle, eager for the fading sun to set fully and the night to claim his body and mind when he slept.

After a time he reined in Midnight to a slow gait. Off in the distance he heard sounds. Not usual night sounds of owls or coyotes or whispering tree branches but something different. He dismounted and tethered his mare, then walked on foot toward the sound. With a hand on his gun, he came up behind a man taking an ax to the line shack, destroying what was left of it. He found most of the boards holding up the shack in a haphazard heap, looking much like a stack of fire logs ready to be lit.

Clint startled the man. "It was you all along."

Sonny turned abruptly, ax in hand, with sweat pouring from his brows. He cursed and tossed the ax aside.

Clint cursed right back at him.

"It's not what you think, Clint."

"I doubt you can talk your way out of this one, Sonny. I had my suspicions, but you were really the last person I thought would bring harm to this ranch. Tell me the truth. Were you behind all of it?"

Sonny winced. Then nodded slowly.

Furious, Clint's temper flared. He couldn't get Tess off his mind. How she'd almost died at Sonny's hands. He shouldn't give a damn now, but he did.

Clint rushed him, grabbing his shirt collar and pulling him up until they were nose to nose. "You left Tess out on the range to die!"

"No, no. Not that. That was an accident. I was only fixing on breaking up a line shack and then I saw the wolf. I shot it. I didn't see her horse rear up and throw her. I swear to you I didn't."

"Like hell. I don't believe you."

"No one was ever meant to get hurt. I wouldn't have put that gal in danger for the world."

"Why not? She in on it with you?"

Sonny gave a quick shake of the head. "No, it was all my doing. She had nothing to do with it."

Clint released him and Sonny sagged back on wobbly legs. The man looked painfully weary and overwrought. At this point Clint didn't know what to believe. "Was it revenge? My father didn't name you in the will, is that it? You hated him, too?"

"I never hated your father. He was my best friend. We grew old together here in Hayworth."

Clint grunted. "He didn't leave you anything for your trouble."

"He paid me handsomely through the years. Enough so that me and the missus plan on moving off Hayworth land once I carry out Hoyt's last bidding. I gave him my word I'd stay on to see this through."

"I'm losing my patience, Sonny. Unless you want a fist in your jaw, quit talking in riddles."

"It was your father's idea, Clint. He asked this of me and I…couldn't refuse him."

"I may hate my father, Sonny, but even I can't believe he'd want you sabotaging the ranch. He loved this place too much."

"He loved you more."

Clint stared at him, his mind clicking, spinning ideas in his head.

Sonny sat on the pile of wood that used to be the line shack. "Sit down, Clint. And wipe that snarl off your face."

Clint didn't argue. He sat.

"Listen, your father and me quarreled about the wisdom of this, but Hoyt insisted. He made me promise. He said if you were to come back here, I was to make trouble on the ranch." Sonny reached into his pocket and lifted out a piece of crumpled paper. "He gave me this list."

Clint grabbed the list and began reading.

"Make equipment disappear, burn down the feed shed, cause a water leak in the tank, tear down fences, rustle cattle over to Granger Holloway's place." Clint stopped reading the list. All of the things that had happened on the Double H recently were listed, and there were a few more "crimes" to come. Still puzzled, he looked at Sonny for answers. "Did my father take a hard blow to his head?"

Sonny lifted his lips, the first sign of relief he'd

seen on his face. "The day he died your father was alert and in control of his mind as he'd ever been. He spelled out everything I was to do, and in what order. He gave me detailed instructions. He wanted this all to start shortly after his death so it wouldn't look too suspicious when you arrived."

"He couldn't know I'd come."

"He didn't for sure. But he'd hoped."

Clint shook his head in disbelief.

"He did it for you. He knew you belonged on the Double H. He knew you loved this place. And he also knew you'd probably never see him alive again. He'd tried several times to reach you, Clint. You refused to see him."

"I know all that. What I don't get is why'd he put you up to this? That's saying if I buy your story— which is still debatable."

"It's true, Clint. My loyalty has always been to this ranch. Your father knew doing this would be hard for me. But, you see, he'd been overly generous with me through the years, in ways I won't describe to you now. But trust me when I say I owed him his dying wish."

"To sabotage the ranch?"

Sonny nodded. "To keep you here."

"To keep me here?" Clint's voice lifted in astonishment.

"He knew you'd never walk away while the Double H was in trouble. He wanted you to become invested in the ranch. He felt you belonged here. He wanted you to have the ranch, Clint. He owed that much to you."

Clint's anger boiled just below the surface. He spoke through clenched lips. "He destroyed my family…for this ranch. He hurt my mother, broke her heart and drove his only son away."

"Everything he asked me to do here was for you. In his own way, Hoyt is telling you what you meant to him."

Clint drew oxygen into his lungs several times, trying to make sense of this. "That cagey bastard."

"Maybe he was, but he loved you. That's why he only willed you half the ranch. He trusted Tess would never allow you to sell the ranch. He'd asked for her promise and she kept that vow."

"He shouldn't have trusted her with anything. She's a liar and a cheat."

The sun had fully set now and only a few stars lit the sky. The summer air had cooled considerably, but Clint still boiled.

Sonny scratched his head. "I know about her past, Clint. That's one other thing Hoyt confided in me. He loved her. And he trusted her even though she'd come to the Double H under false pretenses. He understood her motives and accepted her."

"So at least that part of her story is true."

"There's more."

"Hell, I think I've heard enough."

"He thought Tess was the perfect woman."

Clint snorted.

"For you." Sonny said.

"For *me?*"

"Yes, for you. He cared deeply for her. And he loved her in his own way, but he wanted to keep her on the ranch, too. It was, I believe, part of the reason he married her. He wanted to give her stability, for one, but he'd always said Tess was a match for you."

Clint's temper flared again, this time uncontrollably. He bounded up. "Damn him," he muttered. "Damn him to high heaven. That man found a way to manipulate me from his grave! Not even his own death could stop him from getting what he wanted! Hell, I almost fell into his trap!"

"Having a good woman like Tess and running the Double H is hardly a trap, boy. Think on that. Think on that a *good long* time." Sonny rose, grabbed the ax, plopped on his hat and faced Clint. "I'm done here," he said quietly, his voice weak, his body spent. "I've carried out my promise. It's up to you now."

He walked toward his horse, then turned back around. "Take it from an old man—don't go letting your stubbornness and pride destroy what you want in life. You and that little gal belong together. I've seen you together. And, remember, there ain't a decent soul who don't deserve a second chance in life."

"You think Tess deserves one?"

"Hell, boy, I wasn't talking about Tess. I was talking about *you*."

Sonny mounted his horse and rode off.

Clint picked up a plank from the pile and flung it with all of his strength, letting go of pent-up frustration. Then he grabbed his gear and made camp, tossing his blanket down, too damn rankled to think about a meal or anything else but the fact that his father had gotten the last word.

Once again.

Chapter Sixteen

"Are you sure you want to do this, Tess?" Tom asked, reading over the papers she'd handed him with the details of her life.

She sat with Laura and Tom in their kitchen, too distraught to spend another night under the same roof as Clint.

"It's time I came clean," she said. "The town deserves to know the truth about me. I can't help another woman like Pearl or run Hoyt's businesses or have the town's respect until I tell my story. I'm counting on you, Tom," she said, then glanced at Laura. "And I think you both should call me Theresa from now on."

Theresa Metcalf had thought she was through running away when she'd left Turner Hill and become Tess Morgan Hayworth. She'd put her past behind her and wanted a fresh start. She'd worked for Hoyt, then married him. But she hadn't been true to herself. She'd been hiding under a false name and identity.

If she'd learned one thing from Hoyt, it was to stand up for herself. But she'd learned another lesson, too. And the blackmailer had helped her realize that she couldn't hide from her past. If she did, there would always be another Smiley Brown around the next turn who could hold her life ransom just by knowing her true identity. She didn't want to live that way any longer. She needed to face the truth, hold her head up high and live her life without fear of being recognized, scrutinized or judged.

She'd earned that right and that freedom. She wouldn't give anyone else the power to destroy her life ever again.

Laura put a hand on her shoulder. "You can always count on us, Theresa. And you're staying here at the house. I won't have you living at the hotel, even if you do own it."

"But I don't want to impose."

"You won't be. Tom will be busy writing your story, and I…could use the company. And some help with Abby."

Even though her heart was breaking, Theresa had to smile. "I'd never refuse helping you with Abby."

"I know. Pretty clever of me, isn't it?" Laura chuckled, and Theresa saw an inkling of the perky, happy woman Laura had been before she'd had Abby.

Tom lifted his head from the notes she'd given

him. "We want you to stay for as long as you'd like. If you ask me, Clint Hayworth is a—"

Laura elbowed him in the stomach.

"Ow!" He rubbed his stomach. Then smiled at his wife. The old Laura was returning and Theresa saw hope in Tom's eyes.

"Tom, be careful what you say. She loves him."

"She's too good for him."

"No, I'm not," Theresa said in a rush. Then she shook her head. "I—I mean," she stumbled with her words, then shrugged. "We both have pasts that have caused us injury."

"So you're not angry with him?" Laura asked.

"I didn't say that. I'm so mad at him you might see steam coming off the top of my head soon."

Laura consoled her. "You need time to think things through."

And recover from the deep ache churning in her gut. Clint had turned her life upside down. He was impossible most of the time. "I know one thing—Clint won't bully me into changing my mind. I won't sell him my half of the ranch. If he wants a fight, he'll get one."

"But that's not what you really want."

Theresa wanted to go home, back to the Double H, where her heart belonged. She loved the ranch, the friends she'd made there—and she still loved Clint desperately.

"No, I don't." She wouldn't give in to her bouts of melancholy. She couldn't allow her heartache to destroy every stride she'd made thus far. "And, Tom, at the end of that article you write for the *Herald,* please put in an announcement that the Hayworth Extraordinary Ladies Partnership will hold its next meeting on Wednesday in the hotel dining room. Tea will be served at three."

"I'll be there," Laura said. "I'll stand beside my dear friend."

"Thank you," Theresa said, appreciating the support. It was a risk but one she was willing to take. She hoped the town would forgive her the deception. She wasn't that weak, frightened girl anymore. She'd do whatever she must to make things right again.

Tom set aside the papers she'd given him and rose from his seat at the table. "Can I get your bags from the hotel now?"

Theresa looked from Tom to Laura, who was nodding her head in agreement. "Yes. Thank you, Tom."

Laura took hold of her hand and squeezed gently. "I'm glad you're staying with us. And you're doing the right thing, honey. I'm proud of you."

That's all Theresa Metcalf Hayworth could ask for at the moment.

Clint sat at the kitchen table, the big house empty and quiet but for Greta slamming cabinet doors and banging pots around.

She slid a plate of overcooked ham, runny eggs and burned biscuits over to him. "Breakfast, Mr. Hayworth."

Clint stared at the food. Then scrubbed his jaw. "Looks good."

Greta slammed down another pan on the stove. "Grits will be coming up."

"Grits? Hell, Greta, I hate grits. You never cook them."

"Hmph."

He craned his neck around to find a deep frown pulling at her expression. "What's eating at you, anyway?"

She waved her arm through the air. "You do not know what you have done sending Mrs. Hayworth away."

"Why do you care? You never wanted her here."

"You are wrong. She is a *goodt* woman."

Clint knew Tess had left last night. He'd gotten a report from Randy the minute he'd ridden up this morning: "Mrs. Hayworth lit out of here with a full carpetbag. She was crying."

Randy had looked at him with accusing eyes. Clint had brushed past him, ignoring that look, telling himself it's what he wanted.

Yet, strangely, he found no satisfaction in her leaving. But she was gone and soon she'd give in to his demands. He'd buy her out and sell off parcels of Hayworth land. "She's a liar, Greta."

"We have all told a lie at one time. That does not make us liars. If we live true to ourselves, then we tell the truth."

"Is she living true to herself?"

Greta gave a sharp nod.

"How?"

"I did not make it easy, no. But she is strong. She honored your father's wishes. She works hard for the ranch. She has helped…many."

"You knew what Sonny was doing, didn't you?"

Greta set a kitchen cloth over her shoulder. She sat down. "I did not know all. When I found out, I *toldt* him to stop, but he *wouldt* not. He told me of your father's plan. Then I see…your father was a smart man."

"You don't mind what he had Sonny do?" Clint pushed his plate aside. Greta had made her point. The food did not appeal. He wasn't hungry anyway.

"No. You are a *goodt* man. Mrs. Hayworth is a *goodt* woman. You *shouldt* be together like you were the other night." She pointed her finger at him. "You will make beautiful children."

Clint didn't need a reminder of the nights he'd lain with Tess. She'd been pliant and giving and generous. The heat they'd ignited on that bed could cause a wildfire. He couldn't get enough of her.

He'd come to admire her, too. She handled herself around the ranch. She kept the books straight and made sure the payroll was met. She had won over the crew. They respected her.

Clint ran his hands through his hair.

Greta's comment about children whipped through his mind. He'd never thought he wanted a family. Lord knows, he'd never thought he'd want to be a husband. Not after the bad example his father had made.

But his mind flashed a scene of Tess holding Laura's baby in her arms. Everything inside him softened at the image.

His mind muddied up and he was sure he needed to clear his head. He left the house in haste.

Leaving behind the bitter taste of Greta's words.

Theresa sat with Laura and Marla in the big, lavishly decorated hotel dining room. It was precisely ten minutes past three. But only three women were in attendance for her second HELP meeting.

Her story had been in Sunday's edition of the *Herald*. Theresa hadn't been about town much since then. But today she had walked toward the hotel with head held high, wearing a high-collared russet gown with white lace at the base of the sleeves. The dress was one of her favorites, making her feel good about herself in a way only a woman would understand. She found that today she needed the extra boost. Several shopkeepers had turned away, pretending not to see her on the streets. Others had just plain veered a wide path from her. Of course, the hotel staff was cordial to her. She employed them. But whispers behind her back were evident.

"Have faith," Laura said. Little Abby slept in a basket beside their seats.

"We can have our meeting anyway," Marla said, taking out the handkerchief Theresa had given her when they'd met here last time. She placed it on the table and stroked over the crimson roses delicately.

The gift reminded Theresa of all she still wanted to accomplish. "Yes, we will have our meeting."

A waitress came into the room, her gaze darting around the empty tables set with china cups and plates. She held a tray of tea and pastries with both hands. "Mrs. Hayworth? Shall I serve the tea now?"

Theresa lifted her chin and smiled. "Please do."

A minute later two women entered the dining room wearing their rose-embroidered handkerchiefs pinned to their blouses. "We're sorry we're late, Mrs. Hayworth."

Laura grabbed her hand under the table and squeezed. Theresa straightened in her seat. "Please have a seat. Tea is just being served."

And another minute later three more females entered the room and took their seats. They acknowledged the others in the room and one by one took out their own handkerchiefs, placing them somewhere on their person where they could be seen.

Several more ladies walked in, their steps tentative.

"Come in, ladies. We're just about ready to get started."

Theresa decided to think of the meeting room as half full rather than half empty. She stood and thanked everyone for coming. "Having you come today means a lot to me, ladies. As you may very well know now, I've made a few mistakes in my life—and the worst of all was lying to people who trusted me. So the first thing I want to do is introduce myself to you." She cleared her throat. "Hello, I'm Theresa

Metcalf Hayworth and I hope you will find it in your hearts to give me a second chance."

Laura interrupted to add, "That's what these meetings are all about—getting a chance at a fresh start. We're all here to support each other as women, right?"

Many ladies nodded and some spoke up, encouraging Theresa.

"We heard what you did for Pearl Cowper, Mrs. Hayworth. It was real decent of you."

"You might've saved her life."

"You can't choose who your relations are, any more than you can choose a sunshine sky over a rain cloud."

"We aren't here to judge anyone."

Theresa's heart opened wider to these women whom she'd feared would judge her harshly. But they hadn't. They'd accepted her. Many might have similar stories to tell, and she hoped that by finally confessing about her life, others would trust enough to confide in the group.

Tom had written her story. He'd outdone himself, his prose and sentiments depicting Theresa's life telling of her struggles with a violent father and an outlaw brother. He'd written in a way that asked for no measure of pity but for simple Christian understanding.

"Is it true, Mrs. Hayworth? You're gonna build a home in town for our meetings? And…a place for women to come if they need help?"

"Yes, it's true."

It had been something brewing in her mind for

weeks now, and once she'd told Laura about it, her friend had become excited by the prospect. She'd volunteered to run the home, something she could do while raising little Abby.

Laura had helped Theresa so much when she'd first arrived in Hayworth that she couldn't think of a kinder or more supportive person to oversee HELP at Home. Laura had dreamed up the name of the house, and Theresa thought it perfect.

Tom had penned the first lines of her story well, entitled Meet Mrs. Theresa Metcalf Hayworth.

Instead of giving in to a blackmailer's demand, she decided her money was better spent opening a home to support and encourage women. The home would be open to those who'd been victims of cruelty and mistreatment. To meet Hoyt Hayworth's widow is to know the real Theresa Metcalf Hayworth.

Tom had started her story from her early child-hood memories, exposing her life for the town's scrutiny. Theresa had faced worse things and she'd bear the weight of her life story if it meant she'd be given a second chance.

She belonged here in Hayworth. This was her home now. "Now, ladies, since we've decided to open this home, let's put our heads together. I'll need your help and suggestions."

After a full hour of discussion, Theresa concluded the meeting, marking a date for the next meeting. A dozen women left the room, buzzing with excitement.

Laura beamed her a smile. "You did it, Theresa."

She had. She felt certain fulfillment now. She'd made the first step in gaining the town's trust. But with their trust or without it, nothing would stop her from building the HELP home. "It's a start anyway."

"Those ladies are so excited they're bound to speak about it. They'll bring their menfolk around. And I betcha the ladies who didn't come to this meeting will regret not being here. They'll show up next time, for certain. They can't help but see the good thing you're doing."

"I hope so, Laura."

Then Theresa turned to take a look at Abby. "The little angel slept during the whole meeting."

"She is an angel, isn't she?" Laura agreed, bending to bestow a kiss in the air just above the sleeping baby's head. She fluffed the blanket up and lifted the basket. "But we'd better get her home before she wails for her supper, which will be anytime now."

Theresa and Laura were just leaving the hotel when they bumped into Sonny Blackstone. He'd come in while they were going out the door.

"Oh, Sonny! Hello."

Sonny had a frown on his face. He seemed shaken and unsure and older than she'd ever seen him look. "Mrs. Hayworth, I need a word with you."

Immediately her thoughts flashed to Clint. "What is it? Did something else happen on the ranch? Is it Clint? Is he hurt?"

Sonny looked at Laura, then back at her. "No, ma'am. Nothing's happened at the ranch. Clint's fine."

"Well, thank goodness." Laura excused herself. "I'll leave you two to talk. I've got to get the little one home. I'll see you there later?" she asked Theresa, waiting for her reply.

"Yes, I'll be there shortly."

Once Laura walked off, she focused her attention on Sonny, her heart pounding hard. Even though Sonny had said all was fine, she didn't quite believe it. He'd come all the way from the ranch to speak with her. "Sonny, please tell me."

He took off his hat and fingered the brim nervously. "It's about Hoyt. And Clint. And you. I have a confession to make."

Clint entered the kitchen, took one look at Greta's burned offerings and exited again. For the past three nights she'd cooked up his favorite meals, burning them just enough to ruin the taste. And each night the *Herald* newspaper article about the illustrious Mrs. Hayworth sat under his nose on the kitchen table next to his plate. He hadn't given Greta the satisfaction of reading it in front of her, but he'd read it. And reread it.

Plain and simple, he missed Tess. The whole damn ranch missed her, the boys clamming up tight when he'd entered the bunkhouse. He'd seen the quick blame on their faces in the moment when they'd first caught sight of him. And once that damn article about her life story had been printed, news about her had spread on the ranch.

They'd all believed her story. They'd believed she'd been a victim. She'd had a tough life. Shooting and killing her brother had been an unselfish act on her part. She'd saved two innocent people that day.

Clint didn't know what he believed anymore. He'd always had a hard time with forgiveness. Had he transferred the blame he felt for his father onto Tess?

Clint entered the parlor and headed straight for the bourbon bottle sitting on the sideboard. He poured the whiskey and gulped it down, his mind in a quandary.

When he heard a knock on the door, he knew Greta wouldn't answer it. She'd taken to doing minimal chores these days, out of rebellion. If she hadn't been like a second mother to him for years, he'd have fired her. But she was just as much a part of the Double H as he was.

And that revelation stunned him. But he didn't have time to think on it. Another sharp knock echoed through the house.

Briskly he walked to the front door and opened it. Sonny stood on the doorstep. "I'm not coming in," he said.

There was look of remorse on his face. "I'm quitting, Clint."

Clint dropped his jaw.

Sonny smiled with finality. "Don't look so glum, boy. I've been meaning to for a while now. I wouldn't leave while your father was alive, especially once he took ill. But it's time for me."

"You've been here so long I can't imagine this place without you. You *are* the Double H, Sonny."

"Well, I appreciate that, I do. But I'm handing you the reins. It's up to you now. I've spoken with Theresa—that's what she wants to be called now. She knows everything. My conscience is clear."

Theresa?

He supposed that was her real name, but he'd always think of her as Tess.

Clint stood there as myriad feelings washed over him. He scratched his head, then took a steadying breath. "I feel like I'm losing a father."

"You ain't lost anything. I'll be around. You're a good man, Clint Hayworth. I'm proud to have known you all these years."

"Same here, Sonny."

Clint wrapped his arms around his old friend and they embraced for a few moments. Sonny backed away, teary-eyed. "I'd best go tell the boys now."

Clint swallowed. He gave Sonny a nod and shut the door.

Not a minute later, another brisk knock resounded through the house. "Sonny, that you again?" he asked, pulling open the door.

But it wasn't Sonny. It was Tess. She stood holding her carpetbag in hand, her chin pointed up, her auburn hair flowing down, wearing a pretty silk dress that brought out the brilliant blue of her eyes. He'd never witnessed anything more beautiful in his life.

Clint's gut clenched seeing her again.

Everything inside him fell into place.

For the first time in a long time he knew what he truly wanted.

"Listen to me, Clint Hayworth. I don't care what you think of me. But this is *my* home, too. I belong here. I love the Double H. And I'm not leaving again. If you want me off this property, you're gonna have to pick me up and toss me off yourself!"

"Is that so?" Clint asked. He looked behind her to the ranch hands that pretended not to watch by the barn and corrals.

"Yes, that's so!"

"Okay, then," he said, picking her up, loving the feel of her in his arms again. He tossed her over his shoulder, his hand holding her steady just below her derriere.

"What are you doing!" she screamed, kicking her feet in the air.

"Hold still," he said. Clint cast a quick look at the knowing, approving faces of his ranch hands before stepping back into the house. "I'm doing what I should have done weeks ago."

Clint climbed the stairs two at a time.

Tess quieted some, her voice mellowed when she said, "What's that?"

Clint entered his bedroom and set her down onto the bed. Then he backed up to look at her. Her hair fell forward. She blew lace ruffles off her face.

He laughed. "I missed you, Tess."

"It's Theresa."

"You'll always be Tess to me, honey."

"What's that supposed to mean, Clint? Don't talk in riddles. I thought you were throwing me off the Double H."

"Why would I do that?"

She narrowed her eyes.

"Okay, fine. I admit it. I was wrong about you. I was wrong about everything."

Tess stood up from his bed. He sorta hated to see that. But he intended to have her there soon enough anyway. Permanently.

"Are you saying you're not going to try to buy me out of the ranch?"

He scratched his jaw slowly, contemplating. "Hmm. Well, that really depends."

"On what?" she asked.

"On whether you agree to marry me."

"Marry you?"

"I love you, Tess. My father was right. You are a perfect match for me. You belong on the Double H. He was right about that, too. Took me a while to figure it out. Made me madder than hell to know he'd tricked me, but—you know what?—I don't care about that anymore. The minute I saw you standing there on the doorstep I realized you and I belong on the Double H. We'll run this ranch together. Marry me, Tess. Be my wife."

Tears sprung from Tess's eyes. "C-could you repeat that? I didn't hear anything after you said you loved me."

Clint grinned and walked over to her. "Do you love me, Tess?"

She nodded. "I do. I love you, Clint."

He wiped the tears from her eyes. "Don't cry, honey."

"But it's just that…I didn't expect this."

He placed his hands around her waist. "Neither did I. Falling in love with you wasn't what I'd intended when I first came back. You weren't who I expected to find living here. I had this image in my head of a greedy widow out to cheat me out of my half of the ranch. I never really gave you a chance."

"No, sweetheart. You didn't. But I couldn't go back on my promise to your father."

"You've had a hard life, Tess. I didn't make anything easy for you. But even through all my anger, I admired you for sticking to your promise."

"Do you forgive him?"

"I'll try, Tess. That's all I can offer right now."

She touched his face, her hand a gentle caress that would heal all of his wounds. "That's all I ask."

He took her into his arms and kissed her soundly on the lips, telling her how much he loved her as he breathed in her scent and stroked her body, willing away the pain he'd caused her. "I'll make it up to you, Tess. I want to erase all the bad things in your life."

She smiled lovingly and kissed him again. "I always knew you were a good man."

"Don't say 'just like your father.'"

"No, sweetheart. I won't. You are your own man. And I've never loved anyone like this in my whole life."

"We'll have a good life here on the Double H."

"I'll have your babies." Then a sudden panicked look crossed her expression. "You want children, don't you?"

Clint flashed a vision of Tess holding little Abby Larson in her arms. He hardly could believe that one day he'd witness her holding their own child in her arms. "Yes, we'll have babies. The sooner, the better, honey."

Clint had never experienced such happiness.

He'd come back to the Double H looking to dissolve a forced partnership with his father's clever widow and instead found trust, love and a partner for life. He could thank Hoyt partially for that and maybe one day soon, Clint would forgive his father entirely.

With Tess by his side, all things were possible.

Epilogue

Theresa stood in her chemise, looking out her bedroom window into the starry midnight sky. She hugged herself, hardly believing that she wasn't the widow Hayworth anymore but Mrs. Clint Hayworth, co-owner of the Double H ranch, the Hayworth holdings, founder of HELP at Home and, most importantly, wife to the person she loved most in the world.

Today had been her wedding day and tonight her wedding night. They'd had a huge gathering on the Double H, with decorations and music and wagonloads of food. It was the wedding she'd always dreamed about. But as she gazed up at the sky, giving a prayer of thanks for all that was good in her life now, she caught a flicker of something right before she turned away from the window.

"Oh, my!" She couldn't believe it. "Clint, are you awake?"

"I'm here, waiting for you to come back to bed. The wedding night isn't over, darlin'."

"But you have to see this. Come quick."

Clint rose and stood behind her, wrapping his arms around her, kissing her throat. "What am I looking at, besides my beautiful wife?"

She placed her finger on the window, pointing to the corrals below. "Look, just outside the shadows."

Clint peered out. "I'll be damned. It's the palomino."

"He's pacing. Right by the corral."

"He's been gone a long time. I never thought I'd see him again."

"But he came back, Clint."

"He's wild. Untamed."

Tess turned to look into her husband's eyes. "Maybe he is, but he still needs a home. Should we go down to get him?"

"No," he answered. Then he took her by the hand. "Come back to bed, honey. Sunset will be there in the morning."

"Because he knows this is his home now?"

"Yeah, because he knows this is his home now."

She smiled at her handsome husband. "Just like you?"

He took her into his arms and lowered her down onto their bed. "Yeah, just like me."

* * * * *

Enjoy a sneak preview of
MATCHMAKING WITH A MISSION
by B.J. Daniels,
part of the **WHITEHORSE, MONTANA** *miniseries.*
Available from Harlequin Intrigue
in April 2008.

Nate Dempsey has returned to Whitehorse to uncover the truth about his past…

Nate sensed someone watching the house and looked out in surprise to see a woman astride a paint horse just on the other side of the fence. He quickly stepped back from the filthy second-floor window, although he doubted she could have seen him. Only a little of the June sun pierced the dirty glass to glow on the dust-coated floor at his feet as he waited a few heartbeats before he looked out again.

The place was so isolated he hadn't expected to see another soul. Like the front yard, the dirt road was waist-high with weeds. When he'd broken the lock on the back door, he'd had to kick aside a pile of rotten leaves that had blown in from last fall.

As he sneaked a look, he saw that she was still there, staring at the house in a way that unnerved him. He shielded his eyes from the glare of the sun off the dirty window and studied her, taking in her head of long blond hair that feathered out in the breeze from under her Western straw hat.

She wore a tan canvas jacket, jeans and boots. But it was the way she sat astride the brown-and-white horse that nudged the memory.

He felt a chill as he realized he'd seen her before. In that very spot. She'd been just a kid then. A kid on a pretty paint horse. Not this one—the markings were different. Anyway, it couldn't have been the same horse, considering the last time he had seen her was more than twenty years ago. That horse would be dead by now.

His mind argued it probably wasn't even the same girl. But he knew better. It was the way she sat the horse, so at home in a saddle and secure in her world on the other side of that fence.

To the boy he'd been, she and her horse had represented freedom, a freedom he'd known he would never have—even after he escaped this house.

Nate saw her shift in the saddle, and for a moment he feared she planned to dismount and come toward the house. With Ellis Harper in his grave, there would be little to keep her away.

To his relief, she reined her horse around and rode back the way she'd come.

As he watched her ride away, he thought about the way she'd stared at the house—today and years ago. While the smartest thing she could do was to stay clear of this house, he had a feeling she'd be back.

Finding out her name should prove easy, since he figured she must live close by. As for her interest in Harper House… He would just have to make sure it didn't become a problem.

* * * * *

Be sure to look for
MATCHMAKING WITH A MISSION
and other suspenseful Harlequin Intrigue stories,
available in April
wherever books are sold.

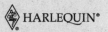

REQUEST YOUR FREE BOOKS!

Harlequin® Historical
Historical Romantic Adventure!

2 FREE NOVELS PLUS 2 **FREE GIFTS!**

YES! Please send me 2 FREE Harlequin® Historical novels and my 2 FREE gifts (gifts are worth about $10). After receiving them, if I don't wish to receive any more books, I can return the shipping statement marked "cancel". If I don't cancel, I will receive 6 brand-new novels every month and be billed just $4.94 per book in the U.S. or $5.49 per book in Canada, plus 25¢ shipping and handling per book and applicable taxes, if any*. That's a savings of 20% off the cover price! I understand that accepting the 2 free books and gifts places me under no obligation to buy anything. I can always return a shipment and cancel at any time. Even if I never buy another book, the two free books and gifts are mine to keep forever.

246 HDN ERUM   349 HDN ERUA

Name   (PLEASE PRINT)

Address   Apt. #

City   State/Prov.   Zip/Postal Code

Signature (if under 18, a parent or guardian must sign)

Mail to the **Harlequin Reader Service:**
IN U.S.A.: P.O. Box 1867, Buffalo, NY 14240-1867
IN CANADA: P.O. Box 609, Fort Erie, Ontario L2A 5X3

Not valid to current subscribers of Harlequin Historical books.

Want to try two free books from another line?
Call 1-800-873-8635 or visit www.morefreebooks.com.

* Terms and prices subject to change without notice. N.Y. residents add applicable sales tax. Canadian residents will be charged applicable provincial taxes and GST. This offer is limited to one order per household. All orders subject to approval. Credit or debit balances in a customer's account(s) may be offset by any other outstanding balance owed by or to the customer. Please allow 4 to 6 weeks for delivery. Offer available while quantities last.

Your Privacy: Harlequin Books is committed to protecting your privacy. Our Privacy Policy is available online at www.eHarlequin.com or upon request from the Reader Service. From time to time we make our lists of customers available to reputable third parties who may have a product or service of interest to you. If you would prefer we not share your name and address, please check here. ☐

nocturne™

The Bloodrunners
trilogy continues with book #2.

The hunt meant more to Jeremy Burns than dominance—
it meant facing the woman he left behind. Once
Jillian Murphy had belonged to Jeremy, but now she was
the Spirit Walker to the Silvercrest wolves. It would take
more than the rights of nature for Jeremy to renew his
claim on her—and she would not go easily once he had.

LAST WOLF HUNTING

by RHYANNON BYRD

Available in April wherever books are sold.

Be sure to watch out for the last book,
Last Wolf Watching, available in May.

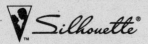

Romantic
SUSPENSE

**Sparked by Danger,
Fueled by Passion.**

The Taken

Tierney Doyle is used to being criticized for
her psychic abilities, yet the tough-as-nails—
and drop-dead-gorgeous—detective has no doubt
about what she has uncovered in the case of a
string of unsolved murders. And Tierney is slowly
discovering that working so close to her partner,
detective Wade Callahan, could be lethal.

Look for

Danger Signals
by Kathleen Creighton

Available in April wherever books are sold.